I0725488

JOSHUA
& CALEB

by

Frank G. Davis

Copyright © 2023
Joshua & Caleb
by Frank G. Davis

Notice of Copyright

All rights reserved. No part of this book may be reproduced or transmitted in any form or by any means, electronic or mechanical, including photo copying, recording or by an information storage and retrieval system without permission of the author, except from the inclusion of brief quotations in a review.

First Edition, 2022 under ISBN: 9798810474913

SECOND EDITION 2023   ISBN: 978-1-954253-56-8

Published by Authors Wild imprint of Van Velzer Press

DEDICATION

This book is dedicated to Gene Carr. Without his enthusiasm for my writing and his assistance in the process, I would never have become a published author.

Thanks Gene

INTRODUCTION

The Sinaloa Cartel—Culiacán, Sinaloa, Mexico

"I tell you the truth, we must strike now. The death of the *pendejo* Carlos has given us an open door to his cartel in Columbia but we must strike now!" said El Mayo in Spanish to the leaders of the Sinaloa cartel. They had gathered together in Culiacán, the founding city of the cartel, to plan their takeover.

El Mayo, also known by his given name, Ismael Zambada-Garcia, stood at the end of the conference table. He was a short man, only 5'9" but that was three inches taller than his predecessor, El Chapo. El Mayo had solidified his position as leader of the Sinaloa cartel shortly after El Chapo was incarcerated in an American federal prison in Colorado. Each of the men present were considered bosses, El Mayo was the boss of the bosses.

He slowly looked around the room at each of the bosses, then said, "If we wait, we risk losing a substantial amount of new business. Worse, if some other cartel is able to move in before us, we risk losing some of our existing businesses, especially in South America. This will not be easy, much blood will be spilled but we must be certain most of the spilled blood will be that of our rivals."

That brought smiles and a few chuckles to the bosses. To a man, each boss had been responsible for many deaths. They looked forward to the opportunity to spill more blood; much more blood. Their cartel was known as the most ruthless of the numerous drug cartels throughout the world. Once El Mayo had taken over, they had expanded beyond drugs. Now they were into human trafficking, the slave trade, the sale of military weapons of every description and even a few legal operations such as casinos. The casinos were also a place to launder the money they made with their illegal businesses.

It was a little over two thousand miles from Culiacán to Washington DC. Joshua Brown had just finished his workout in the hotel's extensive gym facilities. It was the first time he had worked out at a hotel gym that had some decent iron to lift. He enjoyed lifting heavy weights even though the hotel gym limited him to bench press no more than 315 pounds. After lifting three sets of ten reps each with 315lbs he could feel his chest, shoulders and arms pump up from the workout. Now he was ready for a shower and some lunch at one of the restaurants within walking distance of the hotel.

He stripped down, turned on the shower and stepped in. He really liked the programable shower. He had set it to Very Warm for two minutes then it cranked up the temperature to Hot for five minutes, then it dropped to Ice Cold for a final two minutes before warm air flowed over him drying him completely. The first time he used the programable feature he forgot to check the Scent setting.

Apparently, the last person to use the shower had programed the this setting to Spring Lilacs and hadn't deleted the setting when they checked out. Joshua smelled like a flower shop for most of the day. It drew some puzzled looks from passersby.

He stepped out of the shower and was putting on his clean clothes when Caleb interrupted him, *We've got a new assignment, Joshua. The boss wants us in New Orleans the day after tomorrow. They'll be sending you the mission statement. You should be getting it by encrypted email by the time you finish dressing.*

The voice inside Joshua's head was his brother's. It still took him by surprise sometimes to have his twin brother pop up unannounced. He was so glad that at least a part of Caleb had survived. He wished it was all of him but at least the IED that destroyed his body in Kabul didn't destroy his spirit. In some ways it was very comfortable to be able to 'talk' to his brother anytime he wanted. However, there was a lingering doubt that perhaps the psychiatrists were right after all. Maybe it was just a coping mechanism and he couldn't accept the fact Caleb was gone. It was kind of like a multi-personality disorder but not exactly. Caleb didn't take over his body or make him do things he wouldn't ordinarily do. He just 'talked' to him quietly; actually, silently, mind to mind.

Joshua thought of Caleb's spirit as his guardian angel, akin to divine intervention, protecting him in the conflicts he now had to deal with. And his new job had put him in harm's way almost daily.

When Caleb died, Joshua almost died with him. It took him almost a year to recover from the trauma of his brother's death. He received a medical discharge from the Marines and had no idea what he would do with the rest of his life, especially without his brother or his parents. Their parents had passed away within six months of each other while the brothers were in basic training. As many twins, they were exceptionally close. Now that Caleb was physically gone, he had no one to help him through the pain of grieving.

While Joshua was in rehab, a rep from the VA approached him. He said the VA provided training for vets who had been discharged. He just needed to go through a battery of tests to see what occupation he might be good at. His test results caught the eye of a government agency that was looking for people with combat experience. It was a super-secret para-military organization with apparently unlimited funding. They were especially interested in troops that had been associated with special operations like the Navy Seals, Army Rangers or Marine Recon groups. Joshua and Caleb had both been part of the 2nd Marine Reconnaissance Battalion based at Camp Lejeune, North Carolina.

Joshua signed up. Of course, no one knew Caleb's spirit would be tagging along. After six months of intensive training, Joshua was selected for his first mission. It was a feasibility assignment in Nogales, Arizona. After successfully completing the Arizona mission he moved on to a more complicated task involving international players in Portland, Oregon. The last feasibility assignment was even more complicated and took place in Jericho, Mississippi. All the missions were successfully completed. It was now time to move on to even more complicated and highly dangerous assignments. It would start in New Orleans.

DAY 1

<u>New Orleans—Joshua Brown</u>

I checked out of the hotel in Washington DC after breakfast and took a limo to the airport. I'd packed the fancy suit and all that went with it into my duffel. I wasn't sure I'd ever wear it again but it was the first suit I ever bought since joining the Marines. That seemed like a lifetime ago and in many ways, it was a lifetime ago. The only weapons I'd kept with me when I arrived in the nation's capital were the two Desert Eagles, 50 caliber semiautomatic pistols. They were locked away unloaded in separate carrying cases at the bottom of the duffel. All the other weapons I would need, including my War Wagon, would be waiting for me in New Orleans.

The limo dropped me off at the Executive Terminal of the Ronald Reagan Washington National Airport in Arlington, Virginia. The airport is located on the shores of the Potomac River. The main runway extends out into the river on reclaimed land. I had a Marine pilot tell me it was very similar to landing on an aircraft carrier in the middle of the ocean, "There's water all around you until you touch down, then you better hustle to clear the active to the taxi way because there are a dozen planes following you to land."

The limo pulled out onto the tarmac and dropped me next to a C-21, a military version of the Learjet 35A. The C-21 has all sorts of uses, including providing transportation for high ranking military officers. My ride was outfitted for a three-star general who was on assignment and loaned me his ride for the day. The interior looked like the interior of a CEO's office. Actually, I'd never been in a CEO's office but I had seen pictures.

The trip to New Orleans would take about two hours, according to my military pilots. We'd be landing at the Louis Armstrong New Orleans International Airport located 11 miles from the center of the city. I'd use the time to go over the mission statement and 'discuss' it with Caleb.

Once my flight landed, I was picked up by another limo and delivered to the Marriott New Orleans Hotel located on Canal Street only a few blocks away from the Mississippi River. The hotel was adjacent to the French Quarter and within easy walking distance to Harrah's Hotel and Casino.

A bellman offered to take my duffel but I thanked him and said I would carry it myself. I took the elevator to the 24th floor. My room, actually a suite of rooms, had a great view of the river and Harrah's. After I had swept the rooms for bugs (can't be too careful) I spent several minutes looking out the window. I could barely hear the clanging of the infamous cable cars that ran up and down Canal Street. They kind of reminded me of the ones in San Francisco.

I sat down at the desk, opened up my laptop and began planning for my recon mission at the casino. I thought I might wear the fancy suit I'd bought in Washington DC for the briefing.

I decrypted the mission statement and reread it again:

The leader of the Sinaloa cartel, commonly called 'El Mayo,' has called for a meeting with the major cartel leaders in the western hemisphere. El Mayo has proposed a truce between the cartels to discuss how to fairly divide the business of the lately deceased Carlos Hernandez, the leader of the Columbian cartel. The total assets of the Columbian cartel are thought to be in the billions of dollars.

It is strongly believed that this invitation is a ruse to get the leaders of the largest cartels together, kill them and assimilate all of the major cartel's assets as well as the assets of the Columbian cartel.

The other cartel leaders will be expecting some kind of trick. They will be prepared to start a war. Your goal is to prevent that war and arrest all of the cartel leaders who are still alive. This will be our best opportunity to immediately shut down the majority of the drugs that make it into the United States. You will be running point on this mission, however at some point DEA, FBI and local police will need to be brought on board.

We believe the meeting will take place in two weeks in the Penthouse Conference Room at Harrah's Hotel and Casino. A shell company of the Sinaloa cartel is a partial owner of the hotel and casino. Members of the cartel, including El Mayo and his predecessor, El Chapo, have stayed at the hotel frequently for both business and pleasure. They will be very familiar with the facility and it must be assumed they will have some of their people imbedded in the hotel staff. Attached to this file are pictures of the cartel people we think will be attending the meeting with their names or nicknames included. Do your best to memorize as many as you can. It could help you identify the bad guys quickly.

That is all the information we have at the present time. Additional information will be provided as soon as it becomes available. We will text you on the secure line to notify you of any changes.

Good luck and good hunting.

I logged out of my laptop, closed my eyes and leaned back in my chair. *I need to do some recon tonight,* I thought to myself.

What's this 'I' stuff? Caleb thought back at me. *I'm going to be accompanying you on the recon. You need me. I've already memorized the mug shots of every one of the various cartel people.* There was a brief pause then Caleb added, *You'll need a disguise. What about going as a white man? You can make a head mask like they do in those* Mission Impossible *movies. They're so real looking no one would suspect you're black.*

I shook my head and smiled. *I don't have a machine that makes those kind of masks and I can't get one in the next couple of hours. I'm just going to dress in my suit and stroll around the casino and the hotel. If we can manage it, I'd like to get a peek at the penthouse. What do you think?*

I think I'd like to stroll the French Quarter, just to see if Bourbon Street is really as nasty as the stories I've heard, Caleb replied.

Bourbon Street isn't part of our mission but feel free to check it out. I'm going to take a nap and head over to Harrah's around 2200 hours. You're welcome to join me then.

There was no reply from Caleb this time. Maybe he had other spirit business or maybe he headed out to Bourbon Street without me. I set my alarm for 2130 hours, placed one of my Desert Eagles under my pillow and was asleep five minutes later.

I woke instantly as someone was knocking on my door. "I have a package for Mr. Green."

I slid out of bed with the Desert Eagle in my hand. "Just a moment, please." I picked up my smart phone and checked the time: 2120. Next, I checked the image coming from the mini cam I had placed over the door. The cam was very small. You had to know it was there to even notice it. I saw a man in a hotel uniform with a very large suitcase next to him. Actually, it was more the size of the old fashioned steamer trunks. My driver's license, credit cards and passport all said I was Mr. Green, at least until this mission was over. I put the Desert Eagle back under my pillow, unlocked the door and the young man wheeled in the trunk.

"This just arrived from the airport. What have you got in there, gold bars? That's one heavy suitcase," he said breathing heavily. I assumed it was from the exertion of pushing the trunk down the hall to my suite. He wasn't very big. He needed to put on some muscle or he wouldn't last too long at this job.

I laughed it off. "I wish it was gold but it's just product samples." I tipped him a twenty. He thanked me and left, closing the door behind him.

I put the trunk on the bed. The kid had been right. It felt like it weighed a ton. I typed in the combination that allowed me to unlock it, then open it up. It contained all kinds of electronics gear which I would use to bug the cartel rooms. There was also a wide variety of weapons: two Uzi Pro Machine Pistols with six magazines, one disassembled Barrett XM500 sniper rifle with two mags of ten 50 caliber BMG rounds, four Glock 19 semiautomatic pistols with six extra mags of 15 bullets per mag of 9mm ammo and two additional magazines with 33 bullet capacity, each Glock came with a detachable sound suppressor, several 200,000-volt Talon 200 stun guns, flashbang grenades, mace and on and on and on.

As I took inventory of all the equipment in the case, I sensed Caleb had joined me. *Looks like there's gonna be a war, bro. Any nukes in there?*

"None I can see so far," I answered out loud. "But I noticed there are gas masks and canisters of gas. I think it may be what Carlos used to knock us out at the battle of Jericho."

So when are all the troops supposed to show up? Caleb asked. *We got enough weapons to arm a platoon.*

"Tonight it's just you and me. We'll check out as much as we can, then decide how much help we'll need," I answered as I picked up one of the Glocks, field stripped it, put it back together, chambered a round, clicked on the safety and tucked the weapon into the waistband in the back of my pants.

I locked up the trunk and placed it out of sight in back of the closet and placed a tell on it so I could see if anyone had been snooping after we left. I armed the motion detector and placed another tell on the door, then turned and walked down the hall to the bank of elevators. It was show time.

Recon at Harrah's—Caleb Brown

I was seeing through Joshua's eyes as we walked the few blocks from our hotel to the casino. It was cold, colder than usual for late February. When I'm bonded with my brother, I feel everything he feels. Right now, we're feeling like he should've worn a heavier coat, a pair of gloves would have been a plus. We were both glad he had put on a wool newsboy hat.

We entered Harrah's through the casino and began a casual grid-search pattern. There were tons of slots as well as every table game ever invented. The place was jammed with players of every race, sex and religion. Well, maybe not too many believers except those who believe they are bound to win eventually. We call those people delusional.

We spent most of the search checking out the staff. Not so much the dealers and pit bosses but security people and cocktail servers. Some of those women were more scantily attired than the ladies I saw on Bourbon Street.

We took the better part of an hour in the casino before heading into the adjacent hotel lobby. There was a cocktail lounge just off the lobby that gave us a good view of people coming and going to register at the hotel or to checkout. Joshua ordered a Coke Zero and some peanuts and we spent half an hour just watching the crowd.

We hadn't had much exchange but finally Joshua asked me, *Recognize any one?*

I answered back, *Quite a few, actually. I counted at least fifteen people from five different cartels. Ten of them were from the Sinaloa.*

Were any of them bosses? he asked.

No, just soldiers. Two of them were women. I recognized one of them as being associated with Carlos' cartel. She was posing as a cocktail waitress. The other one was a dealer from another Mexican cartel. Her name is Rosita.

Really! You remember the names of all those people from the pictures in the Mission Statement?

Of course I do. Don't you?

Joshua frowned a bit before he answered, *Actually, no I don't. Maybe a few of the bosses. There were over a hundred pictures attached to the Mission Statement. Do you mean to tell me you recognize all of them and even know their names?*

Yup. That's the truth, I answered.

Joshua paused for a beat, then said, *Don't take this the wrong way, bro but I don't remember you having a photographic memory.*

You're correct. I didn't but now I do. Maybe it's one of the perks of being a spirit. When he didn't respond right away, I asked, *You okay, Josh?*

Yeah, I'm fine. I was just thinking how much money we could win playing Black Jack with you counting cards for us.

He finished his Coke Zero, stood up and walked to the registration counter.

"May I help you, sir?" asked a very attractive young woman of color behind the counter.

"Yes, miss, you can. My name is Clarence Green. I represent one of the top ten investment companies in the world. I'm looking for a brochure that shows what your rooms look like. Specifically, the suites and penthouses."

Joshua's voice was low and he gave the woman a small smile as he handed her a business card he'd printed up on our computer a few minutes before we left our hotel.

"Of course, Mr. Green, my name is Simone," she said as she checked the business card. "I can help you with that." She unfolded a full color brochure that showed all the different rooms the hotel offered.

Joshua scanned the pictures, nodded his head and smiled again then asked, "How many penthouse suites do you have?"

"We have three penthouse suites," she answered then asked, "What days would you be staying with us?"

"During Mardi Gras week. I'd like to rent the largest of your penthouses."

"Oh, I'm so sorry. All of the penthouses are already booked for that week. However, we still have some very nice suites available."

"Thank you, Simone but I'm afraid a suite won't do. My company is planning on having several parties and business meetings during that week and only the largest penthouse would meet our needs." He paused then said, "Perhaps we could postpone our meetings to the week after Mardi Gras." He paused briefly and then added as if an afterthought, "Are the penthouses occupied now?"

"No, Mr. Green. We had a last minute cancelation and they aren't currently occupied," she answered.

"Would it be possible to take a quick look at the penthouses? I'd love to take some pictures to show to my bosses that Harrah's penthouses are worth postponing our meetings for a week."

She smiled, nodded her head, looked at her watch and said, "My shift is over in about half an hour. If you can wait, I would love to show you our penthouses."

"That would be fantastic." He smiled warmly, then began to frown. "Are you sure you have the time to take me on the tour? I don't want to inconvenience you."

Thirty minutes later, Simone met us in the lounge. She was still wearing her Harrah's uniform but she had let her hair down and if I wasn't mistaken, had sprayed on Coco Chanel. That had been one of my favorite perfumes when I still had a body with a nose that could detect such delicious scents. But I could 'smell' it because Joshua could smell it. I noticed his nostrils flare, which was a sign he was beginning to dig Simone. I also noticed she had a very athletic build; the type Joshua and I had been attracted to in our younger days. *Down boy! She's coming on to you. You don't have time for romance.*

Mind your own business, Caleb. I'm only getting close to her to get more information.

Yeah, right. Who you think you fooling, boy? I said in my best southern drawl.

"Are you ready, Mr. Green?"

"Yes Simone but please call me Clarence."

Oh boy! Here we go. Professionalism out the window, I thought to him.

There were express elevators to the penthouses that could only be accessed with the suite key card. It felt like a rocket launch as it accelerated from the lobby. Simone seemed to lose her balance and bumped against Joshua.

"Sorry, Mr. Gr…Clarence. I don't use this elevator very often. I'm not used to how fast it moves."

The elevator isn't the only thing moving fast, Josh. Watch yourself, Stay focused... on the mission.

On the ride up, Simone told 'Clarence' each penthouse had its own dedicated express elevator. She also mentioned there was a helicopter landing pad used by celebrities who wanted to avoid being mobbed in the hotel lobby by us common folk. There were separate entrances to all three penthouses from the landing pad. Lastly, she mentioned it was possible to interconnect all three penthouses for very large groups. All three suites could accommodate a total of seventy guests.

At the hotel's top floor, the elevator came to a stop and the doors opened directly into the penthouse lobby. Soft lighting came on as the door opened and music began to fill the room. It was a very spacious room with floor to ceiling windows that revealed a fantastic view of the lights of New Orleans and the ships moving up and down the Mississippi. There was a balcony large enough for at least twenty people to sit in very comfortable looking chairs and sip high-dollar adult beverages. Sitting at the bar were two very large men who eyed Joshua suspiciously.

"Clarence, let me introduce you to our penthouse security team. This is Roberto and Manuel. Once this penthouse is occupied, one of them will be at the elevator entrance on the main floor and the other will be stationed in the penthouse lobby. They check everyone who enters or leaves the penthouse to make sure there are no party crashers. They will be with us as we tour the facility."

"*Buenas noches, señores,*" said Joshua.

The men nodded briefly. Manuel said, "We speak English." He was scowling as he said it.

Joshua looked closely at him and asked, "You look very familiar, Manuel. Have we met before?"

"No. I've only been in New Orleans for a couple of months. Before that I was…not in the United States."

The penthouse had ten separate bedrooms. Each bedroom had either two queens or one king size bed. Simone said they could easily sleep up to thirty guests in this suite and twenty in the other two penthouses, seventy guests in all. In addition, there were an assortment of conference rooms that could be used by all three penthouses. They came in varying sizes to accommodate as few as half a dozen people up to one that could comfortably hold fifty.

As we moved from room to room, Joshua took numerous pictures. When we had completed our tour of the suites and conference rooms, Simone took us out onto the roof to see the landing pad and to look at the view.

There was a rail that encircled the entire roof to ensure anyone who had over imbibed didn't fall over the side. As Simone and 'Clarence' got closer to the rail she paused. "Clarence, if you don't mind, would you please take hold of my hand? I'm not very comfortable with heights."

My boy took her hand and they slowly approached the rail. It was truly a beautiful sight of New Orleans by starlight. It was cold and Simone began to shiver a bit. "I didn't realize how cold it was up here. Maybe we should go back."

But my man, being the gentlemen our mother taught us to be, slipped off his coat and placed it around her shoulders, then, in what I assumed was an afterthought, placed his arm around Simone's waist and pulled her close so she could share his body heat…yeah, body heat. A second later she placed her head on his shoulder and cuddled up.

Manuel had remained by the roof entrance and watched the couple with a blank stare. After a few seconds his phone chirped. He answered it and said in a loud voice, "Tour's over we need to lock this up and go back to the hotel lobby."

Manuel didn't wait, he turned and walked into the penthouse as Simone and Joshua walked slowly towards the door. He stopped and hugged her, "Thank you so much for taking the time to show me all of this. Could I take you to lunch or dinner sometime soon before I have to leave New Orleans?"

She stood on tip toe and kissed him on the cheek. "Of course, Clarence." She slipped him her business card and said, "Call me anytime."

As we walked out of Harrah's and headed back to our hotel, I couldn't help myself. *What the hell are you doing? You know better than to get distracted when so much is on the line. You're thinking with the wrong head, man!*

Nope, he thought back at me. *She's a fed. FBI or DEA. We need to check her out when we get back to our hotel.*

How can you be so sure she's a fed?

How many hotel employees wear an ankle gun? I saw it when she bumped into me in the elevator.

I thought for a minute, then replied, *Did you ever stop to think she might be from one of the cartels?*

Was she one of the women in the mission statement pictures?

No but that doesn't mean she doesn't work for them. She could be someone new, not on the list yet. What makes you so sure she's a fed?

Instinct.

Instinct? Is that all you got? Are you willing to risk our lives on a hunch?

Yep. I do it all the time. You could be right. That's why I want us to check her out.

We walked in silence for a few minutes. We were still a block away when I thought to Joshua, *You were right, Simone is DEA. Her full name is Simone Cantrell. She's been with DEA for five years and has had exceptional efficiency ratings. She's been fast tracked and last year assigned to undercover ... why did you stop walking?*

How did you get access to all that information?

I paused before answering, then mentally shrugged my shoulders. *I'm not sure. I just thought about Simone and all of a sudden, all this data about her came flooding into my ... I was going to say 'my mind' but that wouldn't be correct. I just knew. By the way, she's not married, has a black belt in Brazilian jiujitsu and is an excellent shot with all types of firearms from pistols to sniper rifles. She also likes long walks on the beach and piña coladas made with Jamaican rum.* I paused again, then added, *I just made the last stuff up to mess with you. The rest is from DEA records. Her home base is in DC but she has been in New Orleans for two months. She started working at Harrah's six weeks ago.*

That's amazing, Caleb. How did you not know you could do that?

I never had the need until now. I also have some unsettling information regarding one of the penthouse security guards. Manuel is the son of the Colombian drug lord you killed in Jericho. He's not too fond of the Sinaloa cartel taking over. He strongly believes he should be the next leader of his father's cartel. He's making plans to take out El Mayo and anyone who supports him. He's a very angry young man.

Don't tell me you found some kind of database that had all that information?

Of course not. For some reason there was something about him that seemed suspicious. I kinda took a peek in his head to see if he was any relation to Carlos the drug lord and all that information just flowed into my head, well not really into my head since I don't really have a head of my own. Maybe a better way to say it is it flowed into my consciousness.

So you can read people's minds?

It appears so. Who knew?

Aren't the people you are mind reading aware someone is inside their head?

Nope. When I'm mind reading no one can tell I'm probing them for information.

How is it I'm aware of you and they aren't?"

Because we're bonded together. That's why we be 'talking' to each other. I can't bond with anyone else but you.

Can you control people's thoughts? Make them do what you want? Or make sure they can't do anything you don't want them to do?

As far as I know, a spirit can't do that. I know I can't do it.

Joshua began walking again. I didn't communicate with him until just before we entered the Marriott. *One last thing. Simone really digs you, man. She wasn't playing you.*

DAY 2

The Marriott New Orleans Hotel—Joshua

I was up early making a few calls to invite a few of my friends to the party. These were people I worked with before, people I trusted and had my back. They were combat hardened Marines. They would be in New Orleans later today.

I had sent Caleb out on a mission to check out nearby hotels to determine where all the other cartel people were staying and how many were going to be attending.

I called Simone and invited her to lunch to see how she was involved in my mission. I didn't confront her over the phone. I waited to do it in person.

The information that Caleb had given me regarding Manuel complicated our mission. I was pretty sure this was going to get very messy, very quickly. If I didn't control the situation, there would be considerable collateral damage. I needed to find a way to nip this in the bud. First of all I needed to find out what Simone knew.

We met at a restaurant called the Tru Tone located in the French Quarter, easy walking distance from the Marriott New Orleans. She was sitting at the bar when I showed up and I sat down on a stool next to her. "Hello pretty lady, do you come here often?"

She looked at my reflection in the mirror behind the bar and flashed me that beautiful smile. "Only to show the tourists where they film some of the NCIS New Orleans TV series. Agent Pride is supposed to own it."

"I thought it looked familiar. Are they still filming the show?" I asked, just to make conversation.

She didn't answer, instead she finished her drink and motioned to a booth in the back of the bar close to the bandstand. The music didn't start for several hours so we were pretty much alone.

When the server came to our table Simone ordered some kind of spicy dish for us to split and a couple of draft beers. When the server left, her smile faded. Before she began to speak, I held up my hand for her to wait. "I have a confession to make. I'm not really Clarence Green. My name is Isaiah Jones and I'm a special agent with a very covert government organization. I'm here to prevent a war between most of the drug cartels in the western hemisphere."

Her eyes grew wide open as I spoke. Before she could respond, I continued, "I already know you're Simone Cantrell, an up and coming agent with the DEA. What I need to know is what do you know about my operation?"

The server brought us the beers and we waited until she left before Simone replied. The first thing she said was, "I need to see your creds before I tell you anything."

I gave them to her and she took a mini-scanner out of her purse and quickly scanned my credentials. While we waited for feedback, she kept one hand under the table. I assumed she had a weapon pointed at my groin which she would use if she didn't like the scan results. A few seconds went by before her scanner beeped. She slid her pistol back into her ankle holster and smiled at me. "What would you like to know, Special Agent in Charge?"

"Please, Simone, just call me Isaiah or Clarence if you prefer," I replied with a smile of my own. "Why are you undercover at Harrah's?"

"I've been tasked to keep an eye on Manuel. He's the son of the deceased Colombian drug lord. We know he's up to something but we aren't sure what it is. A CI from the Colombian cartel warned me he was coming. El Mayo, the current leader of the Sinaloa cartel, has rented all three of Harrah's penthouses the last week of Mardi Gras. We're sure something is going down between them during that time. We're just not sure what it is? Any ideas?"

I read her in to the classified program and gave her a quick description of what we thought was going to happen. DEA and the FBI were expected to be brought on board within a few days. "I'm the designated lead on this mission and as soon as we get a little more information from … from one of my CIs I will bring everyone on line. Feel free to tell your boss all about the operation but none of the details can be shared until that meeting."

The server brought our food and it was really good. I love spicy Cajun food. In between bites, I asked her, "You mentioned El Mayo is staying at Harrah's the last week of Mardi Gras. How long does Mardi Gras last?"

She finished chewing, swallowed and took a sip of her beer before answering. I noticed beads of sweat forming on her forehead. The food was indeed spicy. After a second sip of beer she replied to my question with a question of her own, "Have you ever been to a Mardi Gras in New Orleans?"

I shook my head. "Never had the pleasure."

She asked a second question. "Are you a Catholic?"

"Nope," I answered. "I was born and raised Southern Baptist. Is that important?"

She pushed her plate of food away, taking a break from the spice, took another sip of beer and answered, "No, not really, I just wanted to know how familiar you might be with Mardi Gras."

"Just assume I'm a newbie."

"Okay, newbie. The words 'Mardi Gras' are French for Fat Tuesday. Fat Tuesday is the day before Ash Wednesday, which, for Catholics, is the first day of Lent. Lent begins a time of sacrifice and fasting that continues for over a month ending up on Easter. In New Orleans, Mardi Gras is celebrated for two weeks. That celebration is people going nuts. Traditionally, on Fat Tuesday good Catholics ate as much as they could to prepare for the fasting that would follow. In NOLA, that evolved into two weeks of not only gluttony but also drunkenness, carousing and debauchery. The number of pregnancies more than doubles during those two weeks. Adultery is not considered a crime or grounds for divorce if committed during Mardi Gras. Celebrations begin two weeks before Fat Tuesday and builds in intensity. During that time there are more than eighty parades throughout the city. El Mayo will be staying the last week, checking out on Ash Wednesday. His reservation is for fifty people plus an undisclosed number of other 'guests.' He indicated he will be arriving by helicopter."

When she finished her Mardi Gras tutorial, Simone got all serious. "Isaiah, I've got one more question, then I'll leave you alone … Are you married?"

I laid my fork down and looked her in the eyes and replied, "Would it matter?"

"It absolutely matters. If you're married we had our last kiss last night."

"And if I'm not married?"

"If you don't piss me off, there might be more kisses."

After lunch, we went our separate ways. I headed back to the Marriott to 'hear' what Caleb had found out about the cartels.

How was lunch with Simone?' he asked when I returned to our room.

It went well,' I answered. *The DEA knows the Sinaloa cartel bosses will be visiting New Orleans the last week of Mardi Gras. But they weren't aware the other cartels will be meeting up with them. They don't know if Manuel wants to join forces with Sinaloa or to wipe them out for trying to take over his late father's empire. What did you find out about the other cartels?*

Well bro, I discovered I now have a plethora of skills I never had before.

So how much is a plethora, two or three new skills?

No man, it means so many new skills I can't count them all. Let me tell you about a very important new skill that allows me to acquire all sorts of secret information, both from humans and, (there was a sound of laughing in the background, and I thought I detected a drum roll) *I can get any and all information stored on any smart phone, iPad, laptop, desktop and mainframe computer ever built. It's just freakin' amazing. No secret is beyond my grasp. All I have to do is ask and it will be made known to me instantly.*

When I didn't respond enthusiastically, I detected he was pouting. *Go ahead, test me if you don't believe what I just told you,* he thought back at me, a hint of irritation in his 'voice.'

Okay, Mr. Smarty Pants, give me the names of the top fifty Sinaloa men coming to Harrah's. I want them sorted by most important to least important, the dates they will arrive, the name of the place where they will be staying and how they will arrive.

Immediately, I heard the sound of a printer. That shouldn't happen, I don't have a printer in my suite. I did a quick check of the room. I saw a very expensive laser printer sitting on the work desk next to the hotel's desktop computer.

As I walked over to the printer, I could feel Caleb gloating. Everything I had asked for was neatly printed out, beginning with El Mayo and working down through his twenty bosses and ending with his soldiers. Before I could comment, the printer started up again and presented the names of the cartel's cooks and security personnel. I noticed the security people were those responsible for guarding the penthouse. One could only guess what the soldiers were for.

I owe you an apology, Caleb. This is really miraculous. Could you do the same for the five strongest cartels?

Of course, Master, your wish is my command. Immediately, the printer began spitting out sheet after sheet of incredibly revealing data on the five cartels. I couldn't thank Caleb enough for the information but he interrupted me with a deep, resonate voice. *From now on, Master, please address me as Genie. And Genie may only grant you three wishes. You've had two wishes granted already. You have only one more wish available. Choose wisely.*

I started cracking up. I started laughing so hard I had to sit down, tears were streaming down my cheek. I hadn't laughed so hard in years, maybe decades. He was truly my brother, we were a team again, blessed by God.

I'll throw in a freebie, Josh. Simone is doing her own snooping. She's been looking to see if you were married. Watch out, bro. She's on the hunt!

Later that afternoon, the friends I had invited to the party showed up, all with new identities except for Sarge, Mark Riley's wonder dog, who had saved my life at Jericho. All three of them were former active-duty Marines who had served in Afghanistan.

Mark and Sarge were a team. Sarge would find the IEDs and Mark would disarm them. Mark was awarded the Purple Heart for being wounded in action and the Silver Star for inventing a way to detonate IEDs from the air using cheap drone helicopters and laser triggers. Sarge had also been awarded the Purple Heart for being wounded saving his handler from certain death from a Taliban soldier. He was awarded the Bronze Star for his courage under fire.

The third Marine who joined us was an American born, Vietnamese lawyer named Pham Bin Minh who was a sniper during his war. He handled legal matters as well as he handled his Barrett XM500 sniper rifle.

All of us had been Master Sergeants during the war, including Caleb. All of us had killed people during the war when we had to. That included Sarge, the largest German Shepard I had ever seen. To his friends, he was a handsome specimen who was very affectionate and loved donuts. To his enemies or enemies of his friends, he was death and destruction. He saved my life by ripping off the testicles of a man who was one second away from murdering me. That man was Carlos, the Colombian cartel leader.

Our suite at the Marriott New Orleans had two bedrooms, one with a king size bed and the other with two queen beds. Mark and Pham took the room with the queen beds, I slept in the king. Sarge slept anywhere he wanted, although he seemed to favor the couch facing the entrance door as our first line of defense. Since Caleb was a spirit he didn't sleep but Sarge seemed to sense he was with us.

DAY 3

Arrest Warrants & Battle Plans—Pham

After a good night's sleep, we met for breakfast in the suite's main room. At 0800 hours, room service delivered our breakfast. The young lady who wheeled the food cart into the room stopped abruptly when she spotted Sarge lying on the couch. "Pet's aren't permitted to stay in the hotel rooms." Her voice sounded a little shaky.

Mark and I replied almost in unison, "He's a therapy dog, not a pet."

"I'm sorry, but during Mardi Gras pets are not permi-"

Sarge slowly climbed off the couch and walked carefully toward her. She seemed to freeze as Sarge strolled up to her and sat down only inches away. He leaned forward and gently began to nuzzle her hand. She didn't move at first, just stared at him looking into his large soft brown eyes. She couldn't help herself. She leaned down and began to stroke the top of his head. Sarge leaned against her as she continued to pet him. "Is he really a therapy dog? He seems so friendly. I guess it wouldn't hurt if he stays with you. I can just pretend I didn't see him. I won't mention it to anyone."

She stood, placed our food on the table and noticed there was a side order of bacon. "Would you mind if I fed him a piece of bacon?"

"He'd love it if you gave him some bacon," answered Mark.

Sarge gently took the bacon from her hand, chewed it up in three bites and licked her hand to thank her. She looked very happy and promised to bring us all breakfast tomorrow.

When she closed the door behind her, the three men turned to look at Sarge. Sarge stared back, barked once and jumped back up on the couch and closed his eyes.

"Sarge, you're such a charmer," I said as he began to snore softly.

When I finished my breakfast I began the process of requesting federal arrest warrants for numerous cartel members. I had no idea there would be so many. They were being charged with multiple offenses, including murder, drug trafficking and illegal entry into the United States. Joshua had produced volumes of records of crimes committed by each individual listed from several of the well know cartels. It would take me at least a week to prepare the requests for warrants.

Joshua told us he would be meeting with the DEA and FBI in the afternoon to read them into the mission and work on what he referred to as a battle plan with assigned responsibilities.

Taking a break from the arrest warrants, I planned to spend the afternoon searching for a good place to set up a 'hunting blind.' When I began sniper training, I asked my instructor what was the most important thing a sniper needs to do. He answered, "A sniper needs to have a line of sight to the target at a 'reasonable' range."

When I asked him what a reasonable range would be, he told me he was sure it would be less than a mile but probably be over a thousand yards.

Before we broke out to work on our individual assignments, Joshua got us together for a status update.

"It looks like it's going to be a war if we don't do something to prevent it. Here's what I believe is the Sinaloa plan. El Mayo wants to get as many of the major cartels in a conference room as he can and kill them. His goal is to take over all of the drug action in the western hemisphere. We don't know exactly how the killings will take place but it seems most likely he would prefer to get it done as quietly as possible to prevent any police interference.

"I think he would likely use gas or poison to either kill them on site or knock them out and transport them to some remote area for the actual killings. My CI says El Mayo has no intention of absorbing them into the Sinaloa cartel, he has to kill them to prevent any rebellions after Mardi Gras. I think this will take place on Fat Tuesday, the last day of Mardi Gras.

"Other CIs have said the invited cartels believe this is a trap and they will be prepared to resist whatever El Mayo's intentions might be.

"El Mayo will be prepared for their resistance but I don't believe he is aware of Manuel. Manuel is planning to assassinate him for not allowing him to run the Colombian cartel after the death of his father. He has no interest in forming any alliances with the other cartels. Since he is part of Harrah's penthouse security I believe he will attempt to booby trap the conference room and kill as many Sinaloa bosses as he can, before the other cartels even arrive.

"So this is what I see needs to be done to accomplish our mission:

"First, we need to stop Manuel from killing El Mayo and his bosses. I believe he wants the killings to be a flash-bang affair. He wants the world to see his vengeance on the Sinaloa cartel for not recognizing him as the new Colombian cartel leader. He wants it to be a blood and guts killing to show the world how strong he is. It would also be a message to the other cartels to keep away from his turf.

"The most likely way to accomplish his goal is to blow up the conference room as soon as the Sinaloa move in. As one of Harrah's penthouse security, he can place his explosives whenever he wants without anyone being aware of the bombs. He would have to detonate them before El Mayo's people sweep the room."

I interrupted. "I think it is highly unlikely that El Mayo will step into the conference room until the room is swept. I would be surprised if El Mayo will even show up at Harrah's until the last minute."

"Good point, Pham. You may be right. We need to check it out," replied Joshua. "In the meantime I would like Mark and Sarge to sweep all the Harrah's penthouses to see if Manuel is storing the explosives either in one of the suites or somewhere else within the hotel. Start with the penthouses. If you don't find anything, check out the landing pad on the roof then move on to the rest of the hotel; storage areas, empty rooms, those kind of places."

When Joshua had finished, Mark put the Therapy Dog vest on Sarge and the two headed out to check out possible explosive cache locations.

I put on a coat and hat (It was cold outside!) and began my search for potential sniper sites. I walked over to Harrah's with Mark and Sarge and took the elevator to the roof to check out buildings that would be tall enough to get a line of site on the floor-to-ceiling windows in the large conference room. I took my range finder to get an accurate distance to my target.

There were two tall buildings a little over a thousand yards from Harrah's that lined up with the conference room as well as the helicopter landing pad. I took the elevator down to street level and headed to the first of the potential sites.

Sniffing for Explosives—Mark and Sarge

We left Pham at the bank of elevators and began walking around the huge lobby area to get Sarge familiarized with the hotel. Several people approached us and asked if they could pet him. Since being a Therapy Dog was an important part of his cover, I encouraged him to tolerate all the contact. Actually, I think he really enjoyed all the attention. We had gone through some extensive training and when I would command 'Therapy,' he was a very docile animal who let people pet him. When I commanded 'Search' or 'Destroy' he was very, very different.

We wandered around the hotel just getting the layout of the place and then began a grid search one floor at a time. We'd walked up all the stairways and took every elevator, except the express elevators to the penthouses, then doubled back and began walking the hallways walking slowly as we passed each room.

I really didn't expect to find anything in the guest rooms but for the sake of thoroughness we went by every room. To my surprise, on the sixth floor Sarge sat down in front of the door and looked over his shoulder at me. He smelled explosives!

I recorded the room numbers of all the rooms Sarge identified as having explosives. There were six in all and we'd only covered half the guest rooms. I contacted Joshua and asked what he wanted me to do.

A young woman in a Harrah's uniform joined me ten minutes later in front of one of the suspect rooms. She was accompanied by two large security guards. She introduced herself as Simone, a friend of Joshua.

When the guest opened the door he looked confused. "Explosives! We don't have any explosives, just some fireworks we plan to shoot off during Mardi Gras."

Simone told them they weren't allowed to have fireworks in the guest rooms, it was considered a fire hazard.

The security guards confiscated the fireworks from all the rooms and told the guests they could pick them up when they checked out of the hotel. One of the guests asked how we knew they had the fireworks but by then Sarge and I were long gone.

Getting the DEA and FBI on Board—Joshua

"Good afternoon. My name is Isaiah Jones and I'm the Special Agent in Charge from Homeland Security. I will be leading this operation. During the last week of Mardi Gras, we believe we will have the opportunity to capture all the major drug lords in the western hemisphere."

That got their attention. I went on to explain what we believed was going to happen and how best to prevent a bloody war between the major cartels and mitigate any collateral damage to guests and Harrah's Hotel and Casino.

We discussed the proposed assignments for the DEA and FBI. We also discussed local police involvement.

I informed them we had federal arrest warrants for over a hundred members of the five major cartels.

My closing comments were: "Ladies and Gentlemen, this is the opportunity of a lifetime. If we do this right we can put all the major drug lords in prison for the rest of their lives. If we do this right we can stop the vast majority of illegal drugs entering the United States. In addition, it will shut down the other crimes they are involved with such as human trafficking, murder for hire and money laundering operations. We may never get this opportunity again. Let's make this happen!"

I stood by the door as they all left the conference room. Caleb had been in my head for the entire meeting. *Well done, my man. Our mama would have been proud to hear your presentation.*

I shook the hand of several of the last people to leave, they seemed very upbeat about the possibilities. *How would you rate the audience, Caleb?*

The older, more experienced troops were skeptical but willing to follow your lead. The young ones want to take names and kick ass. They were definitely pumped. Speaking of being pumped up, Simone was hanging on your every word. You're her hero now. Better watch yourself. Speak of the devil, here she comes.

"Well done, Special Agent in Charge. That was a very impressive presentation. Would you be available to meet with me later tonight? I have some additional information regarding Manuel and other members of the Colombian cartel. Maybe we could talk over dinner?"

Oh Lord have mercy! She's planning her attack on you. Tell her no. Tell her you're going to be busy. Don't let her get you alone.

"I'd love to have dinner with you, Simone. What time is good for you?"

Man!!! Are you even listening to me?

"Why don't you come to my apartment at seven? Let me make you dinner. Do you like French food?"

"I love French food. I'll see you at seven. I'll bring the wine."

I could sense Caleb hadn't been kidding. He was really worried about me getting involved with Simone and not staying focused on the job. But I knew I wasn't distracted. My instincts were telling me she was a key to making this mission successful.

Caleb had disappeared for the moment. But it was important for him to join me when I was with Simone. I needed his lie detector ability.

Dinner with Simone—Joshua and Caleb

Why would you want me to join you for dinner with Simone? I don't want to be in your head when you two get all lovey-dovey. That's just sick, man, protested Caleb.

There won't be any lovey-dovey business tonight. I'm going to ask her some questions and I need you to determine if she's telling me the truth, I answered. *She may not be lying but I don't think she's telling me the whole truth.*

Wow bro! Really? Do you think she could be on the side of one of the cartels?

I'm not sure but my instincts tell me I need to vet her more carefully before I reveal any more of our plan. Are you willing to help me with this?

Of course, Josh. That's what I've been trying to do. And Josh, one more warning.

What's that? I asked.

Make sure she's not packing her ankle gun.

We arrived at Simone's apartment promptly at seven. I had bought a bottle of Chardonnay. She answered the door looking spectacular. She was wearing a simple black dress with a low-cut neckline that showed a modest amount of cleavage. I had to force myself to stay focused on her face. She took the wine from me and set it on the dining table then turned back, grabbed me in a not-to-gentle hug and kissed me passionately. Without conscious thought, I kissed her back.

Caleb was instantly in my mind. *No lovey-dovey business my ass!!! You got to get your hormones in control, dude.*

I hadn't realized I had lifted her off the ground in our embrace. I gently lowered her until her feet touched the floor and stepped back. "That was some greeting!"

She smiled at me and said, "Think of it as the before dinner appetizer." She took the bottle of wine into her kitchen and deftly removed the cork and poured us each a glass. She raised her glass in a toast. "To dessert," she said as she clinked her glass to mine.

I'm not staying for dessert, Caleb protested. *Hurry up and get to the questions. I've got somewhere to be.*

Where? I asked.

Anywhere but here, bro. Anywhere but here. Two good things; she's not packing any heat and the two of you will be alone as soon as I leave.

I could smell the aroma of the dinner cooking on the stove and Simone turned her back on me to check on the food. No weapons that I could see and her dress was snug enough that a gun or even a knife would be visible. She was barefoot and as Caleb had pointed out, there was no ankle gun on either leg. However, I remembered he had said she had a blackbelt in Brazilian jiujitsu. I felt relatively safe.

Dinner was great, she was an excellent cook. She complimented me on my choice of wine and we managed to drink the whole bottle as we ate. When we were finished with the meal, I helped her clear the table. She left the dishes in the sink and we went into her living room and sat down on the couch, facing each other.

She had been smiling all the way through dinner but her expression changed to serious. "I guess it's time for you to start grilling me about the things I haven't told you."

Caleb, are you getting this?

It's a surprise to me too. Just let her talk. We need to know how honest she will be with you.

"So, what have you been keeping from me?" I asked casually.

"Let me start by saying everything I've told you so far is the truth. I just haven't told you the whole truth. Nobody knows the whole truth, including the DEA."

She paused for a moment and took a deep breath, "Manuel is my half-brother. We grew up together in Bogota in our father's mansion. Carlos was my father but my mother was not Carlos' wife. When we were teenagers, Carlos' wife had my mother killed. She was a very jealous woman and believed Carlos loved my mother more than her. So she gave orders to the cartel soldiers to kill my mother and me. I managed to escape with Manuel's help.

"When Carlos found out about what his wife had done, he went insane. I think it was true; he loved my mother more than her. He killed his wife in front of Manuel who had begged him not to kill her but to send her away. But he wouldn't listen. Manuel told me he had tortured her and finally cut off her head with the large knife he always carried with him."

She paused as Caleb said, *All true. Josh. So glad you pulled the plug on Carlos.*

Not me, Caleb. It was Sarge who bit off his johnson and related equipment. He bled to death from the wounds.

Then why did you blow his eyeballs out?

It just felt like the right thing to do.

Simone continued, "Manuel made sure I escaped from his mother before she could kill me but he stayed in Bogota. He sent me to America, he changed my name to Simone

Cantrell, gave me some cash and left me on my own. He told me never to attempt to contact him again. In spite of what Carlos had done to his mother, he wanted to be the one to run the cartel. He was planning on killing his father someday as revenge for his mother then take over the cartel, but someone got to him first."

"How did you end up with DEA?" I asked.

"It's a long story, the short version is that I was hanging out with some unsavory people and was picked up in a drug bust by the DEA. I was lucky. When they found out I wasn't using or dealing they were going to let me go, however one of the agents noticed my passport was Colombian and he assumed I knew something about the cartel and threatened to throw me in jail if I didn't tell him what he wanted to know.

"I was scared to death of being locked up for the rest of my life so I started telling him everything I knew. It led to some significant drug busts and the agent was promoted and took me on as a confidential informant. I got paid for the information I gave him. Unfortunately, a year later the agent was killed in a raid.

"I had met several of the agents by then and went to his boss and asked if I could continue as a CI. He did a background check on me. Someone, probably Manuel, made me look squeaky clean. My records showed I had a BA from a university in Bogota and spoke Spanish, English and French. That last part was true at least.

"The boss offered me a position as a trainee. He was able to get me American citizenship a year later. A year after that, I was Special Agent Simone, working on the Colombian cartel task force.

"A few months ago, Manuel contacted me. I was working undercover at Harrah's registering new guests into the hotel. I hadn't spoken to him for almost eight years. He told me what he was planning to do and that I owed him my life. He knew about this huge cartel meeting and wanted me to get him a job where he could get access to the penthouses. He'd been working security for about a month when you met him on the tour as Mr. Clarence Green."

Damn! I didn't see that coming. I guess I should have dug deeper, said Caleb.

"Can you tell me his plans?"

"I would if I could but he never shared the details with me. Only that he was going to take out El Mayo before the meeting began."

She's telling the truth, Joshua.

I asked one more question. "Is there anything else you can tell me about Manuel?"

She thought for a minute then said, "I don't know if this will help but he has a commercial pilot's license. He got his private pilot's license when he was sixteen but he was flying a couple of years before that with the cartel pilots. By the time he got his commercial pilot's license he was flying everything from business jets to helicopters."

I sat up straight. "Do you know what type of helicopters the cartel had access to?"

"They had six or seven choppers, all the same. I think they were named after one of Donald Duck's nephews. Let me think … Louie? No that's not it … I remember now. It was Huey!"

I 'heard' Caleb 'shouting' in my ear, *Bingo!!! That's it, Josh. That's how he's going to attack El Mayo. With a chopper. Well, it's Lovey-Dovey time, bro.* In his best Kingfish imitation, he 'said,' *I'z gonna leaves ya now.* And he was gone.

Dessert was well worth waiting for.

DAY 4

<u>The War Wagon Returns—Joshua</u>

The day began with room service. The same young lady, her name is Patricia but she prefers to be called Trish, wheeled in a cart laden with great smelling food. Sarge bounded off the couch when he saw her, wagging his tail. He barked just once but had the biggest dog smile I had ever seen.

As Trish began serving us at the table, Sarge sat quietly watching her every move. After everyone had been served she took an extra plate from the cart. "May I give Sarge a plate?" she asked Mark.

"What's on it?" he asked between bites.

"I mentioned to one of the cooks we had a therapy dog staying with us," she replied. "He made a point of serving him a good breakfast. There's ham and bacon, a few pieces of steak and a little sausage."

Mark looked at Sarge, who couldn't take his eyes off Trish as she stood there with his plate in her hand. "I think Sarge is getting more meat than I got," Mark grumbled. "Go ahead, Trish. Let him chow down.

Instead of rushing to gobble up all of the food, Sarge licked Trish's hand first. She petted him on the head as she said, "You're welcome big guy."

Then Sarge cleaned the plate in nothing flat.

After Trish left with the cart, Sarge jumped up on the couch, and with a full belly, promptly went to sleep.

Joshua was looking at his phone. "I just got a text. The War Wagon is waiting for me at the airport. Anyone want to go with me to pick it up?"

Both Pham and Mark raised a hand while the other hand continued to shovel food into their mouths. Sarge looked up when he noticed the hands waving, barked once and began searching for his therapy vest.

We took a cab to the airport and were directed to a secured parking area where they kept the vehicles that were air-shipped. I paid the cab driver and we walked over to the entrance. I showed the security guard my credentials and the transport papers for my ride.

We all did a walk-around to see what new features had been added. They'd added a second roof mounted mini-machine gun and more ammunition storage. The rocket launchers were the same but they'd added more rockets. I'd been told they had increased the power of the diesel portion of the hybrid drive and a second electric motor had been added. One motor drove the front wheels and the other drove the back which improved mobility. The armor plating had been improved but it looked like the bullet resistance windows were the same as before, the same for the run-flat tires.

The interior had all the comforts of home. A new feature was the weapons operator's station. One person could simultaneously control all of the weapon systems using a very sophisticated fire control computer. If the operator was incapacitated, the driver could use a voice command to activate auto-fire. Once activated the auto-fire feature automatically returned fire to incoming attacks.

Another new feature was attack drones. They were fired from the rocket launcher and could pursue aerial targets at very high speed. They could be used for surveillance or to destroy airborne targets.

I noticed the security system had been upgraded. Anyone who attempted to breach the War Wagon once the system was active would receive a shock equivalent to a 250,000 volt stun gun. That level of shock would leave the attacker unconscious for the better part of an hour. When they regained consciousness, they would experience acute pain throughout their body for several hours. It was a very effective deterrent.

I decided to take the War Wagon on a test run. We headed out to a remote bayou area about 25 miles southwest of the city. The locals called the area The Voodoo Bayou. I was glad we were going during the day. Even during the day it was kind of spooky. I'm not superstitious but I wouldn't want to be out here at night, even if I was in the War Wagon.

We found an uninhabited place a little way from the swamp land. We went off road for about five miles and out of sight from the highway to put the wagon through its paces. Pham took the weapons operator seat and familiarized himself with the controls. When he felt comfortable with the setup we made a couple of high-speed bombing runs.

The ground was firm enough and we cranked it up to a little less than a 100 mph. The terrain map said we had about 10 miles to play with and play we did. Pham 'cleared the throat' of both mini machine guns and lit off a couple of rockets just to make sure he knew how everything worked.

We'd stop after every run and let Sarge out to chase any poor creature he could find. He'd chase them down and then let them go. He never killed unless Mark ordered him to.

Pham also fired off one of the three attack drones stored onboard. He used it to watch Sarge as he chased swamp creatures. It became a game of hide and seek for Sarge. He hid in the tall grass until the drone was almost on top of him then he would bolt to a different hidey hole. When the game was over we retrieved the drone and continued our joy ride.

After an hour of scaring any swamp creatures in the area, Pham said he was satisfied. Sarge gave a few barks to indicate he was also satisfied and jumped up on the console between the two front seats to get a good view out the front windshield for the drive home. We wrapped up our play time and headed back to town, stopping at the Navy armory to replenish the ammo supply, refurbish the attack drone and refuel the diesel. Then we dropped the War Wagon off at a secure facility and took a cab back to the hotel.

Mark and Sarge headed out to Harrah's to continue their search for possible explosives. Pham, after hearing about Manuel possibly attacking the cartel meeting by helicopter, selected what he considered the best sniper position. He left our suite a few minutes after Mark and Sarge. That left me alone with Caleb. We took care not to reveal him as my CI. I have all the confidence in the world that Pham, Mark and Sarge would follow any orders I give them. Perhaps, I should include Simone in that group as well. However, we weren't ready to tell them that my dead twin brother was alive and well living inside my head.

What's new, Caleb?"

Lots of things, not certain you have the time for me to brief you. You all busy scaring gators down in the bayou and all. Everybody else gets to go joy riding in your tricked-out ride. You even invite the dog but give no never mind to your own brother.

Are you sulking? Why are you sulking? You're a part of me. When you want to be with me, you're with me. We're like one person. I don't have to invite myself to go joy riding.

Well, when you say it that way, I guess I shouldn't be complaining. Would you like to hear what I found out about the other cartels?

Of course. Without your intel, this mission has no chance of being successful.

Aw shucks, bro. You be apple polishing me now.

Just tell me what you got, Caleb.

Okay. Each of the five cartels El Mayo is targeting are staying in separate hotels. Most of them have already arrived. The Sinaloa are covering all the costs for the meetings. That includes hotel expenses, transportation, bribes paid to get them into the United States and entertainment. We're talking about hundreds of thousands of dollars out of the Sinaloa banks for each cartel, probably close to a million for all of them.

When Caleb paused for a moment, I wondered what was coming next. *You want to know where Sinaloa is getting the funds to cover all these expenses?* he asked.

Of course, I replied.

If you promise to invite me to go joy riding in the War Wagon I'll tell you.

Oh for crying out loud! You're invited to ride in the War Wagon any time you want. Happy now?

Yes I'm ecstatic! They're going to recoup their expenses by hitting all of the other cartels' banks. Actually, each cartel has several banks or places where they stash their wealth. With the majority of their leaders here in New Orleans, as well as the soldiers needed to supply them with protection, the people who remained at home to guard the wealth aren't trained soldiers. It will be a turkey shoot to get rid of them. Each cartel is bringing about fifty people. Assuming ten bosses per cartel and another twenty for aids and personal security that leaves around twenty people. Those twenty are made up of security muscle. They are tough, ruthless people who enjoy inflicting pain and killing anyone who gets in their way. None of those people will be allowed in the penthouse conference room. No weapons will be permitted and thorough searches will be made of anyone attending. At the present time, no one seems to know where all that muscle will be and what they are going to be doing. El Mayo is bringing about a hundred soldiers to help clean up.

I thought you were into mind reading, I chided him.

I am but apparently I have to have a visual on the person or persons whose minds I want to read. No one seems to know where El Mayo is or when to expect him to show up in New Orleans. All I know for sure is the Sinaloa has brought along several first-class computer people. If I can locate any of them, I will try to do my mindmeld magic and find out how they fit into the Sinaloa's plan.

Well live long and prosper, Doctor Spock.

Ah dude? You've got your Spocks confused. Doctor Spock was a children's medical doctor. Commander Spock is the science officer aboard the starship Enterprise NCC 1701.

I paused for effect then added, *Yes, but Doctor Spock was a real live human being. Commander Spock wasn't real. He was only a character portrayed by actor Leonard Nimoy in an old-time television series. He wasn't real, only the figment of the show's creator, Gene Rodenberry. Commander Spock is kinda like you, a figment of my imagination. I just bumped you up to Doctor Spock who passed away nearly a century ago. At least he had been human, just like you.*

I waited for a reply but it never came. After a few moments of quiet, Caleb said, *Not now Joshua, I've got something cooking.*

I wondered if he was upset with me for riding him so hard. It served him right for all the stuff he said about me not inviting him to go joy-riding. I hoped he would contact me soon.

DAY 5

Continuing Search for Explosives—Mark

We completed our search of Harrah's and except for a few more fireworks, the hotel was clean. The only places where Sarge couldn't get easy access were the penthouse suites and the conference rooms. Joshua suggested we accompany him very early on Day 5. Simone had informed him the people staying in the large penthouse had a family emergency and had to return home two days early. Joshua wanted to use the family's misfortune as an opportunity to plant his bugs. They were the latest generation, small, compact and guaranteed by the manufacturer to be 'completely undetectable or your money back.'

Of course, we checked them out in our hotel suite before we installed them in Harrah's penthouses and conference rooms. Joshua cleared the room and placed ten bugs randomly around the suite's main room. Each bug had both audio and video capabilities and what the manufacturer called the chameleon feature. When they are in their transport cases they are a bright red. Once they are placed in the room being bugged, their color changes to exactly match the color and texture of the surface they are attached to. When they're inactive, a normal sweep of the room would never reveal their presence. When active, their energy signal is so small it wouldn't register on any detection device.

He had Pham and I enter the room and attempt to find the bugs. Visually, we found nothing. With the bugs powered down, we attempted to find them using the most sophisticated detection equipment ever made. We still found nothing.

Once activated, it was the same story. All we heard was very low-level static background noise.

But the real question was how strong was the signal strength?

Joshua had us walk around the room and carry on a random conversation while he moved progressively farther and farther away. He monitored the signal on his control iPad. He could split the display to show thumbnail shots from all the bugs or select to home-in on one or two bugs. After a half-hour, he returned to our suite.

"How did it work?" asked Pham.

"See for yourself," he said as he transferred the output to the 80-inch Vizio flat panel TV. The pictures were extremely sharp and the sound level crisp and clear.

"Did you establish a range limit?" asked Mark.

"Range isn't going to be a problem. I spent a few minutes walking around the Marriott lobby and the picture and sound never diminished. So I went outside and across Canal Street and still got great reception. I think we have a winner. Plan on us installing the bugs late tonight when the security people are gone. Simone will give us access. Mark, I want you and Sarge to sweep the large penthouse and all the conference rooms on the penthouse level.

"We'll go in at 0300 hours and we need to be done and gone in 30 minutes. Any questions?"

There were none.

We were in and out right on time. The security lights gave us enough visibility to plant close to a hundred of the bugs. The concentration was the highest in the three conference rooms, but they were put everywhere: in the penthouses we put them in the main room and all the bedrooms, even the bathrooms and out on the terrace.

While Joshua and Pham were placing the bugs, Sarge and I did a very thorough search for explosives. None were found. That was good news but I knew we would have to keep searching after the Sinaloa moved in. That was going to be tricky but hey, that's why we get paid the big bucks.

When we returned to our suite at the Marriott, Joshua activated the bugs and we were amazed what great coverage we got. Now all we had to do is figure out what El Mayo had in store for the other cartels.

Breaking News—Caleb

It was late afternoon when I hooked up with Joshua. I had been tailing Manuel ever since I left him yesterday. I had to make my brother aware we needed to make significant changes in our plan of attack.

He had been asleep when I connected with him. I knew he had been tied up most of last night but this couldn't wait.

Joshua, wake up. I need to speak with you. No response. I tried again, this time with what would seem to him, me shouting in his ear. **You need to get up. This is very important.**

That did the trick. He awoke with his Desert Eagle in his right hand, quickly scanning the room for the enemy who had so rudely disturbed his sleep. Old combat habits die hard.

It's just me, Josh. Sorry I had to wake you but this can't wait.

He lowered his weapon and did another brief look around the bedroom. When he was satisfied it was only me, he relaxed. *Where have you been? I thought you bailed on me.*

Never happened, I replied. *I've been investigating. I'm afraid I have some bad news, really bad news.*

That got his attention. He climbed out of bed and headed to the bathroom. *Open the curtains, please. It's too dark in here.*

I have no hands, bro. You'll have to do that yourself.

Oh, sorry. I guess I'm still half asleep.

I could 'hear' him washing his face to help him wake up then took a seat on the edge of the bed and said, *I hope this isn't about you getting a ride in the War Wagon.*

I didn't dignify his question with an answer. *Listen carefully. Remember way back when we were in DC you asked me if only good people can become spirits when they die?*

He nodded. I said, *Apparently, I was wrong about that. There are evil spirits as well.*

How do you know that?" he asked.

Because I've spent the last day tracking one. Remember when I left you very abruptly yesterday?

Yes, I thought you were mad at me because I said you were more like Dr. Spock than Commander Spock, he answered.

I gave my best impression of a sigh and said, *Do you really think I'm that petty? Don't answer that. In fact it was like Luke Skywalker said, 'I feel a disturbance in the force.' Something just felt wrong so I went to investigate. It was kind of like homing in on a beacon. The closer I got, the stronger the disturbance became. I didn't want to be discovered so I kept a respectable distance but I was able to get some details. It was a conversation on a spirit level, almost identical to what we do. It was between Manuel and an evil spirit.*

Joshua sat up straight, a hint of fear in his 'voice' as he asked, *Who was the evil spirit?*

There was no way to sugar coat this. *It was Carlos, the Colombian drug cartel leader. He wants Manuel to kill you. He wants that to be the first priority. He knows you are here and has identified you to Manuel. Carlos wants you dead before Manuel takes care of the other cartel leaders. Actually, not only you but everyone who was involved in the battle of Jericho. He doesn't want you all killed quickly; he wants you all to be slowly tortured to death. To be specific, besides you he mentioned Pham, Mark and, as he put it, 'the damned dog who bit off my dick.'*

Joshua sat stunned at what he had just learned. I was even more stunned. Stunned that there were even evil spirits, stunned about what Carlos demanded Manuel to do to our team.

I had one more revelation that I dreaded to share with Joshua. However, I had no choice but to inform him. *He also wants Manuel to kill Simone. He wasn't happy that Manuel had helped her escape. When he tried to explain that he was trying to keep his mother from killing her along with her own mother, Carlos just shut him down, shouting all kinds of obscenities at him.*

I could see the expression on my brother's face. Some might have called it a poker face, devoid of all emotion, But I knew that look, it was one of determination. Joshua was never going to let any of this happen. And I was with him whatever it took.

In a quiet, controlled voice he asked, *How did Manuel react to Carlos' demands?*

At first he refused to do any of the things Carlos demanded. There were violent arguments between the two. I think Manuel wasn't aware of his father's spirit until just a few days ago. He was shouting and raving like a mad man. All of his soldiers thought he'd gone insane. They all quickly departed the room when he started screaming at a spirit they couldn't see or hear.

What about Simone? Does she know?

No, I don't think so, I answered. *I think Manuel is still trying to decide if his father has the ability to force him to do what he wants.*

I need to get her into protective custody as soon as possible.

What excuse are you going to give her? asked Caleb.

Joshua thought for a moment before answering. *Well, I'm not going to tell her Carlos' spirit is trying to get Manuel to kill her. I think I'll say Carlos isn't dead. That he was only wounded and managed to escape back to Bogota to convalesce.*

So you're going to lie to her?

It's not exactly a lie. Carlos is alive so to speak. His spirit is alive and still just as nasty as the flesh and blood Carlos.

How are you going to explain he survived having both his eyeballs shot out.

I'll say it wasn't Carlos. It was a man who looked like Carlos who'd been killed.

Another lie, replied Caleb.

More like bending the truth. It's only a partial lie, not a complete lie.

Hmmmm. You're good at partial lying. Like when you refer to me as your CI.

I don't want anyone to know about you spirits.

Why not? he chided. *Do I embarrass you?*

Sometimes but to paraphrase the colonel in the movie A Few Good Men, *'They can't handle the truth.' Enough of this banter. Let's get back on point.*

This really complicates the mission, I said. *Did Carlos say how Manuel was supposed to accomplish all this?*

No. I tried to read Manuel's thoughts but his anger overpowered any rational thoughts he might have had. I need to monitor them both very carefully over the next few days. You'll have to do without me until I learn their plans. All this might go away but I doubt it. Carlos' spirit is very strong. His spirit is pure evil and hatred.

Oh darn, well it can't be helped, thought Joshua.

What? I asked.

Well, I was going to invite you for a joy ride in the War Wagon tomorrow but you're going to be too busy.

How can you joke with all this going on!!! I thought-screamed at him.

I'm not joking. I was planning to take the War Wagon out tomorrow and have you join us. It was the least I could do. Maybe next time. He turned away quickly in an attempt to hide the smile forming on his face.

DAY 6

The Breakfast Meeting—Simone

I was mildly surprised when Isaiah called and invited me to a breakfast meeting. It was going to be just the two of us. He said he had some very important issues to discuss with me. At first, I thought this was just some ploy so we could be together for a little while but as soon as I saw the expression on his face, I knew it was going to be all business.

The dining room in his hotel wasn't too busy and I had selected a corner booth away from most of the others who were enjoying the brunch buffet. He slid into the booth across from me. I tried to lighten the mood a little. "Well hello special agent in charge. What's on your mind this morning?"

"Let's get something to eat from the buffet line first."

We sat down with our plates full of delicious as well as healthy food. I noticed he moved closer to me in the booth. He picked at his food as he spoke in a low voice, "When was the last time you saw Manuel?"

I thought for a minute then said, "I saw him coming off shift last night but I didn't speak with him. Why do you ask?'

"How did he look?"

"I really didn't pay much attention to him. I was checking in a couple from Oregon here for Mardi Gras."

"When was the last time you spoke with him?"

"Okay, Isaiah, why all the questions about Manuel?"

He paused for a bite of omelet as he decided how to answer me. "One of my CIs told me some very troubling information. He said Carlos isn't really dead and he has ordered Manuel to kill you."

I dropped my fork and stared at Isaiah. "That can't be true! There were all those reports of his death. It was a brutal death. I saw the crime scene pictures. He was mauled by a large dog or a wolf and then shot in both eyes."

"My CI says it wasn't Carlos. It was one his soldiers who looked similar to him. He was injured in a massive battle but was able to survive and now he's back running his cartel. He was very angry at Manuel for sending you away to protect you from his mother. Now he's insisting Manuel follow his orders or he will disown him. It's highly likely he has discovered you're DEA and that is the real reason he wants you dead."

I just sat there for a moment in shock, not knowing how to respond. Before I could say anything, Isaiah continued, "Have you had any recent conversations with Manuel? Anything that would indicate he might be considering his father's orders?"

My mouth was dry. I needed to take a sip of water before I could speak. "I last spoke with him two days ago. It was just small talk about the cartel coming in for Mardi Gras. Nothing that involved me." I looked down at my half-eaten brunch. I noticed Joshua had cleaned his plate.

"Simone, I think we need to place you in protective custody until we find out what they're planning. You'll still be part of the task force but I intend to keep you out of harm's way."

Fighting with Manuel—The Spirit of Carlos

What a strange type of existence. I have all these different abilities but I have to use them through my *pendejo* son. He thinks he doesn't have to pay attention to his *papi* any more just because my body is dead. He feels it's his rightful place to rule my cartel. I must make him see he isn't ready yet. I know he has many of my bosses behind him, however he has no idea how to run the business. If he doesn't listen to me, he's going to get himself killed. If that happens El Mayo and his *chingado* Sinaloa cartel will take all of my business. That business is my life, my family. On second thought it's not my life, not anymore. But I can still run my cartel through my son.

I need to find a way to make him follow my instructions but I must do it in such a way he still has the support of my bosses and soldiers. I know I made a mistake contacting him in front of some of my people. I didn't anticipate his reaction. I can't afford to have them think Manuel has gone crazy. They will leave him like rats deserting a sinking ship if they think he has lost his mind. Or more likely, one of my bosses would have my son killed and steal my cartel from us. Manuel must remain strong in their eyes.

From now on, I will only approach him when we're alone. I think I have a plan that will work. I won't let him sleep. I will keep him awake. The *gringos* call it 'sleep deprivation.' I will make him think he is having nightmares, at least in the beginning. I must do this quickly. Time is of the essence. The sooner he gets rid of that cursed *Negro* and his team the sooner we can focus on protecting the cartel. Killing them will be our first priority. That includes my bitch of a daughter who I have discovered is a DEA agent. She must be eliminated or she will bring Manuel down.

Confronting Carlos—Caleb

I had to keep the spirit of Carlos from helping his son. I had no idea how to go about that so I discussed the possible approaches with my brother.

How can we get rid of Carlos? I asked.

You're asking me? I don't have a clue. I don't even have a clue how we communicate let alone how spirits communicate, he replied. *You mentioned you sensed him like a disturbance in the force. Can you expand on that?*

I thought for a minute before answering. *The closest analogy I can think of is a bad smell. Maybe static would be more like it. I was kind of aware something had changed and I could sense where it was coming from. I wanted to find out what was going on so I moved in the direction to where the static was stronger. Eventually, I could hear voices, but they were really distorted. Remember the old analog radios we had as kids? You know, like before everything became digital? If you didn't quite dial into the correct frequency you'd get distorted sound coming out of the speaker. It was like that. Eventually, if I really focused I could make out most of the conversation. I recognized Manuel's voice and the other voice was familiar. It took me a few moments to pin it down, then I realized it was Carlos speaking. Only he wasn't really speaking, at least not Carlos. That was the point when I recognized it was thought-speak, not vocal-speak.*

How long did it take for you to decide you were 'hearing' Carlos? Joshua asked.

Probably less than a second, I answered.

Wow, that long? I could sense the sarcasm.

Hey bro! Things move fast in the spirit world.

So what did you do?

I got the hell away from them before they could sense I was eaves dropping on them.

We were quiet for a few human moments. Then my brother suggested, *I think you should go after Carlos. Shake him up a little. See how he reacts to having another spirit listening to his plans for Manuel.*

I liked his plan. I remembered our Marine drill instructor's motto: When in doubt, attack. Make the first move and see what happens.

Later that night I went searching for Manuel. I found him and his crew turning in for the night. I positioned myself in his room where I had him in my line of sight. He appeared exhausted. A brief probe of his mind showed me he hadn't slept well the night before. I waited to see what happened.

An hour went by and Manuel finally drifted off into fitful sleep. Ten minutes later Carlos arrived. I'm not sure how I knew he was there but I could sense him somehow. I wondered if he could sense me.

Wake up sonny boy. It sounded like he was screaming into his son's ear. Manuel awoke with a start, his gun in his right hand and a flashlight in his left, scanning the room for his attacker.

Relax, mijo. It's just your papi. You don't get to sleep until you promise me you will kill my killers.

Before he could say anything else, I interjected, *Leave the poor boy alone, Carlos. Can't you tell he's exhausted?*

Everything stopped. I could hear Manuel's heavy breathing as he searched for something he could see. Carlos went silent. I waited. After several minutes, Manuel turned off the flashlight and laid down, putting his Glock under his pillow. I waited until he was asleep again.

Hello Carlos. Things aren't going the way you planned, are they?

The room remained silent, except for the gentle snoring of Manuel. I waited another few minutes, then projected, *What's the matter Carlos, cat got your tongue?*

More silence, then in a very weak, almost whisper like voice I heard, *Who are you?*

I'm kind of like you Carlos, the spirit of a dead man, I answered. *Except, I'm one of the good spirits and you're just an asshole. Your plans are never going to work out. The Sinaloa is going to take over your cartel eventually. Why don't you just go back to your grave in Jericho, Mississippi and remain dead. Give up this ghost business and just stay dead.*

I remained in Manuel's room the rest of the night. I never heard another word from Carlos. I knew I had spooked him but deep down I also knew this wasn't over yet.

<u>Who is the Spirit? —Carlos</u>

I must find out who this new player is as soon as possible. I can't let him keep me from using my son from carrying out my wishes. I am running out of time. I need to use a different tactic with Manuel. If I suggest to him that his sister is a DEA agent and she could ruin all his plans, I think he would see her as a threat to him. I know they were very close as children but knowing she is DEA would be enough to convince him to kill her. That would be a start and I could see how this new threat, this so-called Good Spirit, would react. I need to find out if he is all talk or has abilities I haven't yet seen.

DAY 7

New Tactic with Manuel—Carlos

I waited until I could sense that the other spirit had departed before I approached my son. He woke and went through his morning routine, unaware I was monitoring him. He met with some of my bosses and explained why he had been acting so strange the day before. He told them he had a bad headache and it made him a little off. He assured them he was fine. He didn't apologize, a leader never apologizes. They seemed relieved by his words and left him to carry out his orders.

When we were alone, I spoke to him in my softest voice, the way I spoke to him when he was a young boy, *Mijo, I'm so sorry I startled you yesterday.*

He went rigid, quickly scanning the room; he said nothing. I continued, *Please don't think of me as a ghost who has come to haunt you. A miracle has occurred. Our Lord has let my spirit contact you. There were so many things I wanted to tell you about the business before I passed. Unfortunately, I was murdered before I got the chance.*

I sensed he was no longer frightened, now more curious, "Is it really you, *papi?*" he asked softly.

Yes, my son. It's really me.

"How can I know for sure it's you, that I'm not going crazy?"

What if I tell you something you don't know? It would be something very important. You could check it out and see if I'm telling you the truth.

"Okay, tell me," he replied.

Your sister is an agent for DEA. She wants to have you arrested.

He stiffened. "That can't be true. She got me the security job at Harrah's. She knows I plan to kill El Mayo and his bosses."

Yes, she knows your plans but she plans to have you arrested before you can complete your plan.

"I can't believe that. I saved her life, got her a new start in America. She owes me!"

She's a different person now. I want you to check her out and see for yourself if what I say is true. Confront her. You will be able to tell if she is lying. Do it soon, today if you can.

Protective Custody--Joshua

I had spent the night at Simone's apartment. It wasn't supposed to be lovey-dovey time. I just wanted to be sure she was safe before we set up her protective custody. I planned to sleep on the couch with both Desert Eagles close by. Caleb was also with me. Since he doesn't sleep, he kept watch while I slept.

Sometime during the night, Simone came out of her bedroom. She was crying softly. "Isaiah, can you sleep with me? I really don't want to be alone tonight."

Here we go again, thought Caleb.

Not tonight, bro. Strictly body guarding duty.

Yeah, right. I know what kind of body guarding you got in mind.

She took my hand and led me into her bedroom. She was dressed in her pajamas and I remained in my clothes as we laid down in her bed. "Thank you, Isaiah. Thank you for protecting me." A few minutes later she was sound asleep.

In the morning, she made breakfast and we talked about how things were going to be moving forward. I wanted her to move into my suite at the Marriott with the rest of my crew but there were a few things I needed to tell her first.

Over our second cup of coffee I confessed a few things, "Simone, for this mission the members of my team are using different legends. That includes me."

She glared at me for a moment. "So that means you aren't really Isaiah Jones?"

I nodded.

"Are you really from Homeland Security?"

"No but I am from an anonymous government agency."

"Can you tell me your real name?"

"It's Joshua. Joshua Brown. Please only call me Joshua when we are with my team or when we're alone. I can't have any DEA or FBI hear anything except Isaiah."

"How many on your team?" she asked

"Two men and a dog."

"A dog?"

"A very special dog. All of the team are Marines, including the dog. I'll introduce them to you when we get to the Marriott. They will tell you about their specialties when we get to the suite."

Simone packed up a small suitcase and we headed out to the Marriott. When we arrived, Sarge greeted us at the door, his tail wagging and a smile on his face. Simone stood in awe of his presence. "That's the biggest dog I have ever seen. Are you sure he's not a mix of German Shepherd and Shetland Pony?"

Mark answered, "He gets that a lot but he's all shepherd."

I introduced her to both Mark and Pham as Sarge followed her while she walked around the suite, checking it out. "The place is really nice, much better than my apartment. I didn't realize hotel rooms came with a kitchen."

"Wait till you see the gym and spa. It's got pretty much everything," said Pham.

She sat down on the large couch and Sarge jumped up and joined her, resting his massive head on her thigh and staring at her with his big brown eyes. I think it was love at first sight for both of them. Sarge seems to have that effect on most women.

The two men quickly briefed her on their specialties and then we got down to why she was going to be staying with us for a while.

I led off with, "Simone is in our protective custody. We suspect Manuel has discovered she is DEA and may want to kill her for disrupting his plans to take out the Sinaloa cartel bosses. She will continue to work the registration counter at Harrah's hotel but at least one of us will be with her at all times. This may present us with the opportunity to arrest Manuel which would permit us to then execute our original mission, to arrest all of the cartel bosses.

"I told her she now had the room with the king size bed and I would sleep on the couch while she was with us." Sarge barked once. I suspected he wanted to be part of her security team, which was fine with all the rest of us.

We made plans on how things might go down tonight. Simone said her shift started at 1400 hours or 2:00 pm for the those who don't understand military time. She was supposed to get off at 10:30 with a half hour break when her supervisor released her. Nobody thought Manuel would attempt to kill her when she was working the registration desk but we wanted to be prepared for all possibilities. It was more likely he would approach her when she was released for her break or after she got off.

I wanted to make sure we had all our bases covered but I didn't want to include the DEA or FBI on surveillance. It would complicate things if we tried to include them in a separate mission. I thought the three of us plus Sarge were enough to protect her. Caleb was there as well. He was going to be our spotter to alert us when Manuel arrived. He anticipated Carlos would be hovering in the background.

Speaking of Sarge, Mark was able to get one of Manuel's work shirts from the employee locker room. He gave the shirt to Sarge to sniff so he would know his scent and be ready for action. He gave Sarge the command to protect then returned the shirt to the locker an hour before Manuel was to go on duty. Then we waited.

Everyone was in place before Simone arrived behind the counter. She relieved one of the other agents promptly at 2:00 pm. She was wearing a wire so we could listen to and record any conversations that occurred.

After a couple of hours, when there weren't many guests checking in, Simone asked her supervisor for a bathroom break. She left the counter and headed towards the employee locker room.

Heads up, they're coming! announced Caleb. I forwarded his message to Simone and the rest of the team. Then I heard one bark from Sarge. He bolted out of his hiding place and hit the door to the locker room like a linebacker taking out a running back.

There was the sound of a scuffle over Simone's wire. Followed by Simone's voice, "Manuel, what are you doing? Leave me alone!"

"So you are DEA now? How could you set me up after all I did for you. Our *papi* was right about you. *Puta!*" he screamed at her just as Sarge blasted through the door, nearly taking it off its hinges

Where are they? I mentally yelled to Caleb.

There must be a back entrance we weren't aware of. He's got her.

There was the unmistakable sound of two rapid gun shots as the three of us followed Sarge through the damaged door.

It was complete chaos. Manuel was lying on the floor screaming in pain as Sarge executed his favorite attack. The big dog had a death grip on Manuel's groin as he lay at the entrance to one of the bathroom stalls. Standing over him was Simone with her pistol pointed at his head, her uniform pants at half-mast. It looked like he had struck her in the face before she could pull her pants up. Manuel's pistol laid on the floor where he had dropped it after he attempted to shoot Sarge when he attacked.

People were starting to gather at the damaged door but they dispersed when Mark showed his creds and told them this was police business. He ordered Sarge to heel and the big dog let go of Manuel's privates and trotted to stand in the doorway, growling at anyone who attempted to get a peek at the action.

Pham took care of Simone. He took her weapon, the ankle gun, and helped her pull up her pants. She was beginning to go into shock and he took her over to one of the benches in front of the lockers and had her sit down. She was trembling now as Pham called 911 and requested local police and EMT.

I rolled Manuel over onto his stomach and cuffed him. He was in extreme pain and bleeding profusely but I thought he earned it. I could hear sirens approaching and a few minutes later EMTs entered the locker room through the back door. One attended to Simone and the other to Manuel.

The EMT rolled him onto his back. "Wow! What happened to him? He looks terrible. He may bleed out if I can't get the bleeding to stop."

I shrugged my shoulders as I notice several New Orleans uniforms coming through the door. I checked with Simone's EMT. They were getting her ready to transport to a nearby hospital. She said she was okay.

I asked her, "I thought you were a blackbelt in Brazilian Jiujitsu?"

"I am," she answered. "But it's hard to fight with my pants around my knees."

I smiled at her. "I'll join you at the hospital after I finish with the police. Pham will be with you until I show up. You did good, Simone. Sorry you got hurt." I looked close at the cut on her cheek. It was badly swollen but the EMT had stopped the bleeding. I helped her stand and Pham began to escort her slowly to the ambulance.

"Simone?" She turned. "I know it hurts now but I'll tell you what a Marine would say: just rub some dirt in it. You'll be fine in the morning." She smiled and gave me the finger then walked out with Pham.

I knew it was going to be a long evening.

Caleb thought to me, *You got time for me now?*

Fire away. The police can wait, I answered.

We got new problems. Carlos was watching what went down. When he noticed Sarge and then you and the rest of the crew, I thought he was going to shit himself … figuratively of course. Now he's really pissed. This isn't over for him. It's just beginning.

At least with Manuel in the hospital, there's not much he can do until he recovers … if he recovers.

We'll deal with him later. I'm going to talk to the police and then head off to Simone's hospital. I'll probably be there all night. I feel like we let her down. No way this should have happened. It's on me for not checking the outside entrance.

Don't beat yourself up, Josh. She's a tough woman, even with her pants down.

DAY 8

Simone in the Hospital—Joshua

I awoke when a nurse came into Simone's room to check her vitals. It was early morning, around 0630 hours and the sun had just begun to rise. Simone was still sleeping as I stood up from the chair and stretched. When the nurse was finished, I followed him out of the room to speak with him.

"How's she doing?"

"She's doing well," he replied. "The doctor should be making his rounds around ten this morning. He will determine if she's going to be released today but I think there's a good chance she will be going home sometime today."

I thanked him and turned to the uniformed officer standing next to her door. "Any action?"

"Nope," he answered. "It's been a quiet shift. Nobody but hospital staff has entered her room, except for you of course."

"When's your replacement due?"

He checked his watch. "Another half hour."

"Can I get you a cup of coffee?"

He smiled and nodded, then said, "A donut would go good with the coffee."

"You got it," I replied and walked down the hallway to the nurse's station to get directions to the break room.

As I left the nurse's station and was walking towards the break room, I noticed an orderly pushing a gurney into an empty patient's room. I didn't think much of it and didn't bother to look at the person on the gurney until Caleb contacted me.

Joshua, check out the dude on the gurney, it's Manuel!

I stopped abruptly. *No way, man!* I exclaimed. Then turned and walked back toward the room to check the patient myself. Caleb was right. It was Manuel.

Two additional uniform officers were right behind me. The taller one said, "Sorry sir, this man is a prisoner and he's not allowed to have any visitors. You'll have to leave the room now."

"No problem, officers," I said as I left the room and headed for the break room. I got donuts and coffee for the officers and headed back. I gave the officer guarding Simone his coffee and donut and headed to the other officers guarding Manuel.

I introduced myself as Isaiah Jones, SAC from Homeland, showed them my creds and told them I was the one who arrested the prisoner. "How's he doing?" I inquired.

The shorter one thanked me for the goodies and took a bite of donut before answering. "You probably know more than we do. We weren't at the crime scene. We were just assigned guard duty this morning. He's still unconscious from the surgery. We hooked up with him at the ER recovery room. They needed the space so they moved him to this room. Is it true a guard dog almost castrated him?"

The other took a sip of his coffee and added, "I heard the dog bit off his entire package."

"Could be. If true, it couldn't have happened to a more deserving asshole." I started to head back to Simone, then turned and asked them, "What are your orders concerning the prisoner?"

"Nobody gets in except doctors and staff," replied the taller one as he finished his donut. "And we scan everyone for weapons before we let them enter."

"Excellent, gentlemen. Keep up the good work." I turned and walked back to the nurses' station to see if they had anything new. They didn't, so I went back to sit with Simone until the doctor showed up.

She was awake and happy to see me. "When can I get out of this place?"

"I feel fine, just a little headache."

"How's your face where Manuel pistol whipped you?" I asked.

"Didn't need stiches, they glued it together. I can cover up the seam with a little makeup and nobody will notice. It's still a little swollen but it doesn't hurt much."

"Can I get you anything? Coffee? Juice? Breakfast?"

She shook her head. "What I really need is go to the bathroom."

"I'll call an orderly to help you," I said as I reached for the call button.

"Absolutely not. I'm not going into any bathroom unless you're with me. I'm not ready to risk it," she said in a firm voice that told me she wasn't kidding.

I started to help her out of bed but she insisted on getting up without my help. She took my hand and I led her into the bathroom. When she was standing next to the toilet she said, "That's far enough. I can do the rest on my own."

I smiled at her and said, "I have to say that was the most bizarre invitation I've ever had."

As I closed the door behind me on my way out, I heard her say, "Stay by the door, just in case I need you."

86

Manuel Survives—Carlos

I had been with Manuel from the beginning. I had followed him to the hotel, suggested he use the back entrance to the employee's locker room. He demanded none of his soldiers accompany him. He would be the only one to interrogate her. I knew he wanted none of his people to hear that conversation. He wanted no one to know how he helped her to escape from my wife. They might take that as a weakness for his sister. A leader must not be weak. He must not even appear to be weak.

Everything was going as planned. He knew when Simone would be working and waited until she requested a bathroom break. He grabbed her when she was vulnerable, with her pants down but she fought back. When he discovered she was wearing a wire he knew, he was sure she was DEA and had set him up.

I don't know why he hesitated. He should have killed her immediately and made his escape. He waited too long to make up his mind and that damnable dog that ended my life came barreling through the door and attacked him the same way he attacked me in Jericho, Mississippi. He literally ripped off my private parts. I was dying but not quite dead, when the giant *Negro* shot me in both eyes. I was instantly dead, as if a light switch was turned off. No, not a light switch, a life switch. I died but only to be brought back.

I have no idea what happened to me or how it could possibly happen but I intend to have my vengeance on those people and their monster dog. Then we, my son and I, will take control of my cartel. I am sure it is God's will. *Why else would I continue to exist?*

He was waking up, moaning in pain, still groggy from the anesthesia. As he became more fully conscious I 'spoke' to him. *Hello, my son, welcome back to the land of the living.*

His room had very dim lighting. I could see him looking around the room, trying to find who was speaking to him. "Is that you *papi*? Am I still alive?" he asked into the semi darkness.

Yes mijo. Yes to both questions. It hurts, no?

"*Si papi*, it's the worst pain I have ever felt. What happened to me?"

Think hard, my son. Do you remember the beast that attacked you and tried to steal your manhood?

"*Aye, Dios mio*, I remember now. The huge dog that … Did he take my manhood? Tell me, *papi* am I still a man?"

Yes my son. Don't worry. The doctors put you back together but it may be quite awhile before you begin delighting the senoritas again.

"It feels like everything down there is on fire. I don't know if I can survive the pain."

Don't fear. Help is already on the way. Some of my bosses, our bosses, have heard what happened to you. They are coming to save you from the police. They have a special doctor with them who will take away your pain enough for you to get out of this place. You must leave today and take the puta of a sister with us. She will be your hostage until you escape. Then we will kill her and all her friends. We will have vengeance on them all including El Mayo and anyone else who tries to take our cartel from us. Rest now, mijo. I will wake you when they are here.

The Phone Call—Joshua

Simone was resting as we waited for the doctor to visit and hopefully release her. A new uniformed officer relieved the one I had spoken to earlier. I went out and checked to make sure he was the real deal. He satisfied my questions and I returned to Simone. It was 0930 when the call came in.

"Is this Isaiah Jones?"

"Who's calling?"

"I need to speak to SAC Jones immediately. It's very important."

"Before I answer any questions, you need to properly identify yourself."

"My name is Clifford Johnson, I am the assistant director of Homeland Security. I understand someone named Isaiah Jones in masquerading as an agent from my organization. If you're Mr. Jones and you refuse to meet with me, you will be arrested and spend most of the rest of your life in maximum security prison. Do I make myself clear?"

"There is no Isaiah Jones at this number." I promptly hung up on him and called Pham.

I gave him the short version of the short call. He said he'd check it out.

I decided this could be real trouble. I attempted to call my handler to confirm I had received a call from Homeland but he didn't answer. Instead I got some kind of recording informing me "the number you have dialed is no longer in service. Please check the number and dial again."

I called Pham and asked him to set up a meeting with the DEA and FBI. I didn't want this to escalate into something that would scrap the mission.

I kissed Simone on the cheek goodbye and made sure the uniform was alert and left for the meeting. I told her I would be back to take her home after the doctor released her.

As I walked out to my rental car, Caleb thought at me, *Do you think this could be some kind of ploy to get you away from Simone?*

I thought about it but when I couldn't reach my handler, my first thought was Homeland had shut him down.

Isn't your handler supposed to be available to you anytime you call? I thought they didn't answer to any of the other government agencies?

Supposed to be, I replied as I thought about what Caleb said. *You think I should go back in and take Simone even if the doctor hasn't released her?*

It's your call, bro. It just smells like a set up to me.

I stopped walking and thought about it. Less than a minute later I heard the gun shots and started running back to the hospital.

As I ran through the entrance the gun shots had stopped. The elevators were locked down and I ran up the stairs to the fifth floor, both Desert Eagles at the ready. I slowly opened the door a crack and peaked down the hallway. At first, I didn't hear anything.

They're gone, Josh. They got her. Manuel's gone too. I think they used the phone call to get you out of the building.

Why would they want me out of the way? Why wouldn't they just kill me and Simone and be done with it? I thought to Caleb.

Not sure. Maybe they want to take you all out, not just the two of you. I know Carlos wants to take out Sarge for sure, probably Mark and Pham too. He wants his vengeance on all of you. Manuel probably wants it too.

I opened the door and walked cautiously down the hall towards Simone's room. As I got closer, I could see the carnage and hear the cries of the wounded. The others were dead silent. All the police were dead as well as most of the staff. I did a quick look in Simone's room. It was empty but no sign of a struggle and no blood.

As I left her room and walked to where they had Manuel imprisoned, I heard the sound of a helicopter rotor spooling up. A few seconds later they had lifted off. In another few seconds the sound of the rotor was gone. This was the second time I had let Simone down. I promised myself, I would get her back. There wouldn't be a third time.

I was checking out Manuel's room when Pham called me back. I looked at the remnants of a lidocaine bottle and a couple of syringes while he gave me the update. The call was a hoax. There was no one at Homeland named Clifford Johnson. When I tried to call my handler, they had rerouted my call to the recorded message. No one seemed to know how that was done.

I told Pham to postpone the meeting with the feds until tomorrow and get ready to rumble. We were going to get Simone back.

I could hear the police sirens as I walked down the stairs and into the parking lot. The whole hospital was on lockdown. I got into my car and left before the police arrived. If Carlos wanted to kill us all, they would use Simone as a hostage and threaten to kill her if we didn't do what they said. Manuel wouldn't contact me right away, he'd want me to worry about what he and his soldiers were doing to her. When he finally called he would tell us to meet somewhere they could take all of us out without any police interference, probably somewhere on the bayou. After they killed us they'd move on to taking out the cartels. It was a good plan but it wasn't going to work

Fortunately, I had chipped Simone before the fiasco at Harrah's. Each of my team members had been chipped for just this sort of occasion. We didn't have to run around like a chicken with its head cut off. We knew exactly where she would end up and we weren't going to give them the chance to mess with her.

Prisoner at the Tru Tone—Simone

It couldn't have been more than a few minutes after Joshua left I heard the gun shots, lots of gun shots. They were quickly followed by yelling and screaming. We were under attack and I didn't have a weapon. Fortunately, I had changed from my hospital gown into my Harrah's uniform while I waited for my doctor's visit. I sat on the edge of my bed and waited for what I knew was coming. My jiujitsu instructor always told his students your best weapon was a strong body and a calm mind. I took a long slow breath and tried to relax.

The gun shots stopped but the screaming continued. They were the screams of the wounded and the dying. The door burst open and three men rushed in. Two of them did a quick check of the room to make sure I was alone while the third came towards me with a syringe in his hand and a smile on his lips. He reached out to grab my arm to give me the shot but I twisted away from him and hit him in the throat with a knife hand strike. It crushed his larynx and collapsed his windpipe. He couldn't breath and he couldn't scream. Instead he dropped the syringe and fell to the floor clutching his neck. He would be dead in a couple of minutes.

His two accomplices turned to see their partner in crime writhing on the floor. The closest one to me took two quick steps and began to grab me. I feinted as if I were turning to run from him, looked over my shoulder as he closed and back kicked him in his groin. He let out a little scream and joined his friend on the floor.

The third man reached for me and I let him put his hand on my arm before I grabbed his wrist with my other hand and twisted it violently as I turned my body away from him. I was rewarded with the sounds of breaking bones in his forearm as I swept his legs out from under him. He landed on the floor with a resounding thud.

Unfortunately, while I was having fun, a fourth man snuck up behind me, picked up the syringe from the floor and stabbed me in the butt with it before I could turn and defend myself.

Almost immediately, I collapsed onto the floor with my three assailants. A few seconds later I was unconscious.

I woke up when someone slapped me on the face. It was Manuel. He had me cuffed to a chair, both my hands and my feet. I was surprised to see him standing up next to me. After what Sarge had done to him, I was surprised he was alive, let alone standing up and slapping me. "Hello sister. Time to rise and shine."

I looked closely at him and saw the pupils of his eyes were the size of saucers. They'd probably given him lidocaine for the pain and topped it off with coke. One of his toadies was standing close beside him, propping him up.

He turned his head and began speaking as if someone was standing beside him, "Yes, *papi*, I understand we must wait but not too long. I saw them too, your murderers and their pet monster. I too can hardly wait to see them begging for their lives…"

He paused as if listening to someone only he could hear, "What does it matter if she hears me. She will be dead in a few days…" another pause, then "…let them wonder, let them guess. It doesn't matter to me. They will do as I say or suffer the consequences."

I glanced at the man standing next to Manuel. His head was down looking at the floor but I noticed a slight grimace. He was beginning to have doubts.

The good news and there was precious little, was they weren't going to kill me today. The bad news was I could imagine what they had in store for me. *Please God, let Joshua rescue me from these animals.*

The Rescue—Joshua

As I drove back to the Marriott, I spoke to Mark and Pham over the car's hands-free phone. "Do you have a location yet?"

Mark answered, "Yes, boss. She's at your favorite bar and grill or at least close to it."

"There are so many favorites, which one would it be?" I replied.

"The one in the French Quarter," he replied.

"Still not helping. Give me a name," I growled.

"Does the name Tru Tone Bar mean anything to you?"

"Got it! ETA in fifteen minutes. Can you get the War Wagon within a couple of blocks of the place?"

"Roger that. Pham's in route. Out."

Two minutes later, Mark called back. "No joy, boss. There is a very long Mardi Gras parade heading down Royal Street. It's going to go right by the Tru Tone. Orders?"

I pounded the steering wheel and shouted some salty Marine expletives.

Calm down, big guy, thought Caleb. *Just have Pham find an off the street parking place close to the bar and sit out the parade. When it's over we can move in and clean up. It gives you an excuse to wear a mask so you can mingle with the tourists and get close to the bar without Manuel or his people noticing you. Same goes for Mark. You think Sarge would behave at the parade?*

Maybe, I'll let Mark make that call. He can always have Sarge sit in the War Wagon with Pham, I replied.

It's a damn shame.

What's a damn shame?

It's a shame you didn't get one of those Mission Impossible mask makers. You could get a white man's face and mingle with them. You could say all kinds of snappy things, like 'shucks,' and 'gosh all mighty.' Didn't you ever want to be white for a day?

Never! How about you?"

Not in my wildest dreams, bro. I could almost hear the laughter in his voice. His jokes always calmed me down, even when we were kids, he was the joker.

We parked a couple of blocks from the parade route. I bought a mask to wear, an animal mask not the white man mask Caleb suggested, then headed to the parade.

I wasn't prepared for what I saw. There were miles and miles of floats, bands, dancers and women and men wearing next to nothing. How could they do that? It was cold, too cold to wear such skimpy outfits. Caleb suggested they got all liquored up before they got undressed. I saw women tourists lifting their shirts and flashing their breasts in return for a string of plastic beads. I saw a group of naked men running down the street wearing only masks. It was as if everyone had gone crazy.

The floats were amazing. The decorations lavish and unbelievably complex and it seemed it went on forever. Hours later, in the late afternoon, it looked like it was winding down. Thank heavens for that. Just when I thought it was ending, the biggest, most elaborate float I had ever seen came up the street and stopped in front of the Tru Tone Bar. Sitting in a throne at the top of the bar was the actor, Scott Bakula, better known as Pride, the Special Agent in Charge of NCIS New Orleans. He was also referred to as King and he played the part well. Other cast members were on the float throwing beads and trinkets to the fans that surrounded the float. The King stood up and spoke into a microphone. "Ladies and Gentlemen, it's such a pleasure to be back in New Orleans at Mardi Gras. Tonight is special. The cast and I are going to party with y'all right here at the Tru Tone. There'll be music from local bands, dancing, food and drinks, lots of drinks and it's all FREE to our fans. So come join us inside and get this party started. We plan to party ALL NIGHT LONG."

I stood frozen in place. This can't be happening. We have to rescue Simone!

Take it easy, Joshua. This maybe the best thing that could happen. I'll bet you any amount of money Manuel's soldiers won't be able to resist Agent Prides' invitation. They'll make sure Simone is secure, maybe rotate one guard on her every hour while the others party. They'll all be wasted except for Manuel but he's going to be drugged up on pain pills and probably some coke as well. We go in at first light and rescue the damsel in distress and arrest Manuel and his crew.

Again, Caleb was right. We'd take turns monitoring her chip signal. If they try to move her we'll know it. Pham said she's right next door to the bar and hasn't moved since we got here. We got readouts from her chip saying she's okay. I decided to meet back at the War Wagon, grab a few hours of sleep and attack at first light.

The Sinaloa at Harrah's—El Mayo

Our helicopter touched down on the roof of Harrah's hotel at four in the afternoon. Our security people were the first out and scanned the roof to ensure it was safe for the bosses to leave the helicopter. While my aide took care of registering everyone in the party our security preceded us into the largest penthouse suite and did a thorough scan for any bugs or explosive booby traps. Thirty minutes later, the rooms were cleared and the bosses moved into their assigned rooms.

The first helicopter lifted off and a second one landed. This one had our staff people and tech experts on board. While they registered, security now moved to the largest of the conference rooms and began their sweep. It took them an hour and they assured me the room was free from any unwanted devices.

I watched all this on my iPad as I sat in my suite in the Marriott hotel, the one on Canal Street next to the French Quarter. I had arrived two days earlier and had registered as Ruben Salazar, a mid level manager for Dos Equis Beer, in town for the Mardi Gras. I was accompanied by my beautiful young wife, Luz Alicia, and my two sons from a previous marriage, Chuy and Chapo. All three made up and played by my security team. My actual family remained in my mansion in Culiacán, Sinaloa.

There were two bedrooms in the suite. Chuy and Chapo used the one with two queen size beds. Luz Alicia and I slept in the king size bed in the other bedroom, what my real wife didn't know wouldn't hurt her.

The five men who appeared to be the five bosses were actually soldiers who looked very similar to the real bosses. Their appearance would fool anyone except their closest friends. My double looked exactly like me thanks to the plastic surgery he underwent several years ago. He had been an actor and was very good at voice impressions. When he talked, he sounded just like me. I was following El Chapo's example. He taught me to never show up at large gatherings where it was impossible to know if there were assassins waiting for him. The assassins could be *policia* or killers from rival cartels who wanted to take over his business. Using body doubles saved his life on several occasions. My use of doubles saved my life at least once since I took over Sinaloa, perhaps more. I never go anywhere public without them. I consider my doubles valuable assets therefore I have another plan in place as to how to get rid of my rivals. I believe the plan is flawless. I can't wait to see it in action.

DAY 9

<u>Early Morning Recon—Caleb</u>

While the crew slept, I decided to check on Simone. I knew she wouldn't be able to sense me but if I could move my presence close to her, I could read her feelings, her thoughts and her emotions. Thankfully, Manuel and his men had left her pretty much alone. Every few hours one of the female soldiers would bring a bucket and place it between her legs, lower her pants and have her do her business in the bucket, then pull up her pants and take the bucket away to be emptied. They gave her water every couple of hours and one meal, hand fed to her, from a safe distance.

None of the soldiers made any moves on her. She felt they were intimidated by her jiujitsu skills. No wonder, the first three men who tried to capture her had suffered greatly, one died of suffocation when she hit him in the throat, another had his testicles crushed and the third had compound fractures of his right forearm. I would've given her a wide berth myself.

She had finally fallen asleep sitting in the chair around three in the morning as the party next door at the Tru Tone wound down. The soldiers had all done their share of partying and a few had to climb the stairs to their hideout on hands and knees. One even passed out on the stairs. They must have thought they had a few days to make us sweat out what was going on with Simone.

I checked on Manuel while they continued to take care of his injuries. They were extensive and I doubted he'd ever have a good time with a woman again. The cartel doctor had to keep changing his dressing and administering lidocaine to relieve the pain. I gave him a slim chance of surviving his wounds, not that I cared. He got what he deserved. Carlos really didn't care what happened to him beyond needing him to run the cartel business.

After the doctor left him for the evening and Manuel had managed to fall into a drugged sleep, I sensed Carlos was present. *You know he won't survive, don't you?*

He will survive long enough, answered Carlos.

Long enough for what? I asked. *You'll never get your cartel back. When he's gone you're gone too.*

He will live long enough to see the death of my murderers. And when I kill Joshua, you die again too.

So it's really all about vengeance, not the cartel?"

You think you have it all figured out but you know nothing. I will exist long after you're gone and I will guide my cartel, even without my son.

Do you know the Sinaloa cartel is in town and wants to breakup your cartel and divide it among several other drug lords? I knew he knew about El Mayo. I was just pumping him for any tidbit of information I could get from him.

Of course I know but we will stop them, right after I kill Joshua and his friends.

I had enough. I pulled back until I was pretty sure Carlos could no longer sense my presence and waited. I didn't have to wait long. They were on the move before the sun came up.

The Rescue—Joshua

Joshua, wake up. They're bugging out!

I became instantly awake by the sound of Caleb's voice in my head. *Where are you?*

I'm near Simone. Just had an interesting conversation with Carlos but we can discuss that later. Carlos woke up Manuel, had the doctor treat him with lidocaine while one of the female guards was uncuffing Simone from the chair. They're leaving most of the soldiers except for Simone and her guard, the doctor and a couple of men. If I read them right, one of the men is a pilot.

Any idea where they're headed?"

Somewhere south of the city, in the bayou, I think. I'm not reading any specific destination. They still don't realize Simone is chipped. I recommend you follow her but not too closely. Let it play out. I can let you know when they're ready to dance.

Good intel, bro. Everyone is up and ready to go. Give me status updates.

I was driving the War Wagon as we left the parking garage and began to follow Simone's vehicle in the still pitch-dark night. There was at least an hour before sunrise. The roads in the French Quarter were a mess, especially near the Tru Tone Bar. I bet that was a party to remember.

Simone's chip signal was strong and Pham was tracking it and giving me directions to keep us out of sight. We were about a couple of blocks behind and to the side of her street and would remain that way until we reached open country.

They were driving slowly, being sure not to draw attention to themselves. It took us the better part of an hour before we left the city. The sun was just beginning to peek over the horizon and we were now forced to follow in trail formation. There were few cars on the road at that hour but we managed to keep one or two between us and the target vehicle.

As we drove, Pham brought the weapons systems online and set them on standby. Mark and Sarge were in the back. Sarge managed to crawl up on the center console and licked my ear good morning. Then he said hello to Pham as well. He stayed there looking through the front windshield as we got further into open land, approaching the bayou.

Mark was checking his gear, especially his personal weapons, as I got an update from Caleb. I made it look like my CI was calling in with new information.

They're about a mile ahead of you, getting ready to turn off on an access road to a small airport. I spot a few light aircraft, one business jet and a couple of helicopters. I'm pretty sure one of them is a Huey... Yes, I have a positive ID on the chopper. It's a Huey and they are refueling it.

"Roger that. Keep us updated if you can," I said speaking as if I had a human being on the phone.

I drove by the airport access road and turned off on what looked like a dirt bike trail. I switched to four-wheel-drive and pulled up in a small copse of trees to keep out of sight form our target.

Mark asked, "Do you think they're going to start the negotiations or are we busted?"

We didn't have to wait long before my phone started to ring. I answered.

"Is this Clarence or Isaiah or whatever the hell your name is?" It was Manuel but I could tell he was in pain by the sound of his voice. His speech was slurred probably from the meds he was taking.

"Yes. You have my full attention. What are your terms?"

He sounded confused. "Terms? What terms?"

"Terms for your sister's release," I answered.

"Why should I release her? She broke my heart. She set me up. It's all her fault."

"Not really. None of this would've happened if you hadn't tried to take her hostage."

"None of that matters now. I'm dying. The doc says I've only got a few hours to live. I have to prioritize what I need to do before I die. Killing her or you or that *chingado* dog who attacked me aren't high on my list. To be honest, in spite of what she did, I can't bring myself to kill her. If you can find her, you can have her. I've got more important people to kill." He hung up.

Pham was watching a close-up view of the car parked next to the helicopter on the targeting screen. We saw the backdoor of the car open up and Simone, still handcuffed, spilled out onto the ground. There was a single gunshot before Manuel and a man and woman climbed out of the car and quickly got into the Huey. The bird's side door slid close as the rotor began spooling up. The car's back wheels were throwing up dirt as the driver turned the car away from the airport, heading down the access road to the main highway.

I tromped on the War Wagon's accelerator and exploded out of the forest, making a beeline for Simone and the unknown man lying on the ground. By the time we reached them the Huey was airborne climbing quickly and picking up speed as it headed back to New Orleans.

We slid to a stop as close to Simone as I dared. We all bailed out and I ran to Simone who was struggling to get to her feet. Her ankles as well as her hands were still cuffed. Fortunately, as a special agent I had a master cuff key and was able to get the cuffs off of her. I pulled her up off the ground and she jumped into my arms, hugging me like she was never going to let me go. She was trembling as the tears ran down her cheeks. I was hoping they were tears of joy. Then when she kissed me with such passion, she confirmed they were joyful tears.

Mark and Pham checked out the body of the man who had been lying next to her. He had a fatal gunshot wound to the back of his head. He had been the doctor who had managed to keep Manuel alive. Apparently, he hadn't been good enough.

Caleb was in my head. *I hate to break up this happy reunion but our boy Manuel is planning on taking out the Sinaloa cartel before he dies. That Huey he left in is well armed. He's thinking about destroying Harrah's entire penthouse complex. What do you think we should do?*

I think we should stop him.

I think so too. How do you want to do it?

To answer Caleb's question, I turned to Pham and asked, "What's the range on our attack drones? Can we reach the hotel from here?"

"Absolutely not," he answered. "But if we get on the highway and go balls out we might be able get him before he makes it to the city."

We all jumped back into the War Wagon and headed back toward New Orleans as fast as we could go. I was driving, Simone in the front passenger seat, Pham at the weapons console and Mark and Sarge in the back.

Simone leaned over and said in a low voice, "Why would you want to drive with your balls out?"

I smiled. The first smile I had in several days. "It's just an expression pilots use meaning to go as fast as possible. During World War Two, almost a century ago, some fighter aircraft had a feature that could only be used in an emergency. There was a golf ball sized handle on the plane's control panel. When the pilot pulled the ball out, the engine would run faster but only for a short time before the engine would fail."

"So you don't have to take your privates…"

I stopped her. "Nope. Absolutely not."

As the War Wagon broke 100 mph and continued to accelerate, Simone leaned over again and said, "I'm very disappointed."

We were burning up the highway with lights and siren, maxing out at 150. Pham was tracking the Huey and we were gaining on him. "Can we take him out before he gets to the river?" I asked.

"It'll be close. Ask me in five minutes!"

Five minutes later Pham said, "I think we can get him."

"Fire away," I ordered.

The attack drone seemed to explode as it exited the rocket tube and streaked toward the Huey at Mach 2 speed. We watched from the drone's nose camera as it closed on the chopper. They never saw it coming as the missile flew up the engine exhaust nozzle with a thunderous explosion which seem to vaporize the entire helicopter. The debris from the bird fell harmlessly into the Mississippi, some of it barely missing one of the river tour boats.

Manuel was gone and so was the spirit of Carlos. Now we needed to focus on our main mission, stopping the Sinaloa cartel.

<u>What the Hell Was That?!!—El Mayo</u>

It was early in the morning when I was awoken by the sound of a loud explosion. The shock wave from the explosion blew out the picture window in the living room, shards of glass covered the floor. I jumped out of bed and opened the bedroom door in time to see a large fire in the middle of the Mississippi, with roiling black clouds of smoke rising high into the morning sky.

Chuy came running out of his bedroom with a gun in his hand assuming we were being attacked by one of the other cartels. Unfortunately, he was barefoot and cut his foot badly on one of the broken window's glass shards. He fell to the floor holding his foot and screaming obscenities. Chapo was right behind him but stopped when he saw his 'brother' on the floor.

I went back into my bedroom and found my slippers, then ventured out to get a better look at what had happened. At first, I thought two ships were involved in a collision or perhaps a cargo ship had exploded. A strong wind was blowing the smell of the fire toward the hotel. There was something familiar about the pungent odor. It dawned on me; it was jet fuel. An aircraft had crashed or maybe it was a midair collision of two aircraft.

The sound of sirens were everywhere below. Fire trucks were gathering at the river's shore line and I noticed several fire boats already spraying water on the flames. I crossed myself and said a silent prayer for the poor people who had died in the crash. No one could've survived that crash.

Chapo was helping Chuy remove a sizeable piece of broken glass from his foot. I went back into the bedroom, picked up the phone and called the front desk. All I got was a busy signal. I looked down at my 'wife.' She was still in bed. She apparently slept through the explosion. I pulled the covers off of her and shook her. "Wake up. You need to help Chuy and Chapo."

"Why can't I sleep? It's still early," she said as she tried to pull the sheet up to cover her naked body.

"Get up. There's been a very bad accident. Chuy is hurt and I can't reach the front desk for help."

Her eyes opened wide for a second before she jumped out of bed, slipped on one of the white hotel robes and started for the living room.

"Stop!" I yelled. "Put on your slippers. There's broken glass all over the living room floor. And take one of the med kits to fix up Chuy."

After she left, I tried calling the front desk again with the same results. I used my smart phone to contact my bosses to see if anyone else was injured. All their suites were on the backside of the Marriott facing the French Quarter. They were all fine. Most of them didn't even know about the explosion.

The next calls I made were to my people at Harrah's. The penthouse suites were even closer to the river than we were. They reported some limited damage but no injuries. I was informed safety inspectors were on their way to check out if there was any damage to the building. As a precaution, they had shut down the casino and the restaurants and requested the guests remain in their rooms until contacted by a member of the hotel staff.

"Make sure all our equipment in the large conference room is secured before you let anyone in. That's an order."

As I hung up my phone, the hotel phone rang. When I answered, I was told hotel services were sending a representative to our room to check out the damage. They were going to relocate us to another suite on the other side of the hotel away from the damage. They would be arriving in about thirty minutes.

I told them my son was injured and needed medical attention. They said an EMT would join the relocation team to take care of him.

After I hung up the phone, I went into the bedroom and removed my Mission Impossible Mask Maker from the closet. I always created a mask to further hide my true identity when I had to go out in public. I selected a *guero* mask. It made me look like a *gringo*, a young *gringo*, about the same age as Luz Alicia. It took only a few minutes to create the mask and a few more to put it on.

Everyone got dressed and waited for hotel services to arrive.

Returning to the Marriott—Joshua

We drove the War Wagon to the Navy facility to get a replacement for the attack drone installed and then dropped the wagon off at the secure site. We returned to the Marriott in our rental. Well, we almost returned. Canal Street was blocked off due to an aircraft explosion over the Mississippi. The hotel sustained considerable damage, mostly to the picture windows facing the river. We were detoured through the French Quarter and entered the hotel from the rear.

We were met by a young man from hotel services who asked for our suite number. I gave them the information and he quickly checked his iPad. "You're in luck," he said with a smile. "Your suite wasn't damaged by the explosion. We'll be taking you to your floor by the freight elevator in a few minutes. I have a few other guests to assist before we can take you up to your room."

We stepped to the side as he turned and asked another couple for their room number. When they gave it to him, he checked his iPad then informed them their room had been damaged and they were going to be relocated to a different room.

He went through the same process with several other guests before he announced, "We apologize for the inconvenience but your safety comes first. All our regular elevators are currently inoperative. We hope to have them back in service within the hour. But rather than having you wait, we will be using our freight elevator to take you to your floor where another hotel representative will escort you to your room. If you are being relocated, all of your belongings will be moved to your new room as quickly as possible. We ask that you remain in your room until we announce you are free to use all of the hotel's facilities. We thank you for your patience. Please follow me."

We all walked down a hallway to a large freight elevator. There were 34 people in all including a hotel services employee who checked his iPad to determine which floors to stop at. After five stops there were only two groups left, our team, including Sarge in his therapy vest and a party of four comprised of what appeared to be a husband and wife and their two adult sons. One of the sons appeared to have injured his foot.

We rode in silence for a few minutes until the elevator stopped again at the floor just below ours. Before the door opened, Simone said to the young man, "I hope your foot gets better soon. How did you injure it?"

The father turned to Simone and said, "It was caused by the explosion. Our windows were shattered by the blast and he stepped on a glass shard."

"How terrible," Simone said.

The mother smiled. "He's a tough boy. He'll be fine. Thank you for your concern."

The door opened and they stepped out of the elevator. They were met by a young woman in a Marriott uniform but before they walked away, the injured young man turned and smiled at Simone and waved goodbye.

The elevator dropped us off on the next floor, then headed down to pick up more of the displaced guests. As we walked to our suite, Caleb thought to me, *Do you know who that was?*

Which one? I asked.

The father, although I doubt he was really the father.

Who do you think he is?

That was El Mayo!

He didn't look anything like El Mayo.

Of course not. He was wearing one of those Mission Impossible masks.

Oh, for crying out loud!

I scanned him, Josh. It's him. I'm sure of it.

Rethinking Our Strategy—Joshua

I did a quick check of all the rooms in our suites, including the closet with the trunk full of goodies. Everything seemed to be in order and my tells hadn't been disturbed. I also checked the glass in the windows facing the river to make sure there weren't any cracks that could lead to them breaking from the storms that were common in New Orleans this time of year. Mark and Pham did their own checks and everything came up clean.

Simone was exhausted from her kidnapping and escaping from Manuel. She went into the bedroom to change from her Harrah's uniform into some casual clothes she had brought with her when she moved in with us. When she didn't come out of the bedroom, I took a look to see if she was okay. I wasn't surprised to see her sound asleep on the bed. I covered her with a light blanket and turned to leave when Sarge pushed by me, jumped on the bed and laid down next to Simone with his head facing the door. He was in protect mode. I patted his head and softly said, "Take care of her Sarge," then quietly left the room, closing the door behind me.

Pham had turned on the television and he and Mark were watching a local news channel to determine what the police had discovered about the crash. A talking head had introduced an agent from the NTSB who would be in charge of the accident investigation. "Agent Goodwin, can you tell us what you have discovered regarding the crash?" asked the anchorman.

The camera shifted to a close up of the National Transportation Safety Board agent. "We really haven't begun our investigation yet. About all we know for sure is that it was some type of aircraft that was destroyed, not a ship. So far, we haven't found any eye witnesses to the explosion. My team of investigators will be arriving today. I expect it will take several months before we can piece together the details of the crash and why the aircraft exploded. We will report updates on our findings as the investigation moves forward."

The camera returned to the anchor who thanked the agent for his comments. The scene shifted to a shot of Canal Street showing the damage caused by the explosion. "As you can see, Canal Street has been shut down to all traffic until the debris from the damaged businesses and hotels can be removed. Fortunately, the explosion occurred early in the morning well before rush hour. There have been no reports of any deaths caused by the explosion, however there have been a few injuries caused by falling window shards from businesses and hotels. One cable car was reported to have been blown off its rails by the force of the explosion. Now here's Anna to give us the latest on today's Mardi Gras parades."

The scene changed to Anchor Anna. "Good news! None of today's parades have been canceled. However, the explosion has caused some changes to the parade routes, Here are maps of the new routes..."

Mark turned off the television with the remote. "So what's the next step, boss?"

I joined the two men. "I want to set up a meeting with the DEA and FBI. We need to include the NOLA police as well.

I'll make some calls to see if we can meet this afternoon. With Manuel gone, we should be able to give our full attention to planning the raid on the cartel conference. I need to consult my CIs now that the Sinaloa cartel bosses have checked in. I'm hoping to see if they can give us more details on how El Mayo is going to proceed."

I glanced at Pham, his eyes were closed. So were Mark's. They were both up most of the night followed by the adrenaline pumping pursuit of Manuel. Once the adrenalin had drained from their bodies, fatigue had set in big time. "Hey, you guys need to get some rest. That's an order. I'll get you up around noon."

They both got up from the couch and headed sleepily to their bedroom without saying a word. As I watched them go, I realized I was as pooped out as they were. I decided what was good for the goose was good for the gander and stretched out on the couch. I was just falling asleep when Caleb creeped into my brain. *What are you doing man? We got a lot to discuss.*

Go away. Need sleep, Later, I answered. Thankfully, he left me alone.

A couple of hours later, I heard a song in my head:
A little bird with a yellow bill
Hopped upon my window sill.
Raised his cheery head and said
Get your ass out of bed, you sleepy head.

I hated that song when I was a kid. Caleb, who was a morning person, delighted in torturing me with it almost every morning. I found, I still detested it.

Come on, dude. I let you sleep for a couple of hours. It's time for me to update you on what I found out while you were snoring. Then you got to brief our friends at the DEA and the FBI.

I managed to open one eye and look at my watch. I was sure I hadn't slept for two hours but my watch said otherwise. I rolled onto my back and stretched, then noticed a pasty taste in my mouth. I managed to stumble to my feet and stagger into my bedroom as quietly as I could so not to disturb Simone. Sarge's head popped up immediately as I opened the door. He tracked me as I went into the bathroom then immediately went back to sleep. Simone slept through it all.

When I left the bathroom, I felt almost alive and ready to converse with Caleb. *Okay, Caleb. What have you got for me?*

You're going to love this. I confirmed the man in the Mission Impossible Mask was in fact El Mayo. His so-called wife and sons are his security detail. He and all of his bosses are living in our hotel. They came a few days before we did. The bosses who checked into Harrah's hotel yesterday are all body doubles. The soldiers are the real deal and so are the support people. They've rented one of the ballrooms on the first level of Harrah's for a big party for all the cartel people the day before Mardi Gras. They expect several hundred people to show up. It will be a wine, women and song party with live music, show girls and as much drugs and liquor as they can handle. The idea is to soften them up and think maybe El Mayo is really going to propose a plan to share the Columbian cartel's wealth. As far as I could tell, El Mayo knew nothing about what Manuel was planning to do to them. The next day it will be only the bosses from the five major cartels and the Sinaloa. It's going to be the big reveal.

Things got cloudy after that. I got all of that from reading El Mayo's mind but I think Luz Alicia, his pretend wife, was looking for some afternoon delight. So his thoughts got sort of jumbled and confused and finally X-rated. During the confused thoughts, I saw helicopters, gator farms and gun battles. At that point I left the two love birds and went to visit some of his crew at Harrah's. I wanted to see if I could get any idea how they were going to execute the other cartel bosses.

I ran into a big problem. They were doing some major construction in the large conference room but in the smaller conference room they were also doing similar stuff. The construction people were just following orders. They had no idea what they were building or what it was supposed to do. I wasn't able to find the IT people and I needed to have line of sight with them in order to find out what they were planning.

I reviewed the bug videos in both conference rooms. They were great but they couldn't show me what I needed to know. I think I needed to keep visiting El Mayo when he has his pants on. He may not be sharing all the details even with his own bosses. He seems to me he's one of those guys who doesn't share everything with his own people.

I was pleasantly surprised by all the intel Caleb had gathered. I told him I was very excited about the information he provided and wanted to reward him. I suggested a joy ride in the War Wagon. He graciously accepted. Tomorrow we would take a trip to the bayou again.

I also wanted to share all of it with Mark, Pham and Simone (except for the fact that my CI is really the spirit of my dead twin brother). I also wanted to share it with the DEA and FBI. I called my contacts at both agencies and requested a meeting for this afternoon. We were all set to meet at DEA headquarters at 1400 hours.

The Meeting at DEA—Simone

I was surprised that Joshua, aka Isaiah Jones, wanted me to lead the meeting. He said it was a meeting at DEA and I was a DEA agent. I wasn't supposed to dwell on what went down with Manuel and his father Carlos but my DEA boss already knew about Manuel's plan to take out the Sinaloa cartel. I had to tell them something, however the main thrust of the meeting was to prepare for the Mardi Gras gathering of cartels and how to move forward arresting all the players.

The meeting began promptly at 2:00 pm. "Good afternoon, today we will be presenting our plan for the capture of the major drug lords in the Western Hemisphere. First, I want to present a short summary of what went down yesterday and this morning.

"Yesterday, Manuel Hernandez and his father Carlos discovered I was an undercover DEA agent. They kidnapped me…"

"Wait a minute," one of the DEA agents stood up. "Carlos Hernandez was killed almost a year ago in Jericho, Mississippi."

I nodded. "Yes, it turns out his body double was killed. Carlos was seriously wounded but he survived and joined his son to disrupt the Sinaloa meeting. They kidnapped me and attempted to get information about the meeting. I was rescued by Isaiah Jones and his team. Manuel and Carlos escaped in a helicopter and were going to use it to attack the Sinaloa cartel residing in Harrah's hotel. Fortunately, the helicopter exploded before they could reach the hotel. Manuel and Carlos are presumed dead. All that I have told you is classified Top Secret at least until after we make our raid on Mardi Gras. Let's move on to the plan for the raid on the Sinaloa.

"We have received information from confidential informants the Sinaloa cartel plans to kill off all of the major bosses from five of the largest cartels in the Western Hemisphere. When they meet on Mardi Gras those bosses will be incapacitated and taken somewhere outside New Orleans, probably in the bayou, to be executed without a trace. We also believe the target cartels are aware of the Sinaloa's plan and have plans of their own to turn the tables on the Sinaloa. There is a strong probability many, if not all, of the target cartels will unite to counterattack the Sinaloa. None of the cartels want this to go down inside New Orleans. They want this to be a private war without DEA, FBI or local police interference."

One of the FBI agents interrupted, "What's wrong with letting them kill each other? Why should we risk our lives to go to war with these animals. If we try to arrest them they may decide to join forces and take us out first. I hear there could be as many as several hundred cartel soldiers eager and willing to kill us as easily as killing each other."

The room went quiet for a moment. I noticed many of our people nodding their heads in agreement. I wasn't sure what to tell them. I looked over at Isaiah, he stood up and said, "We believe we have a way to capture all of them without anyone being killed, neither us nor them. Let me tell you what we propose to do."

Fifteen minutes later the meeting adjourned. Not everyone was happy with the plan but it was the lowest risk plan we could think of. I thought it was a great plan.

Gatorland, USA—Caleb

The meeting ended about 1530 hours and Pham had brought the War Wagon around in back of the hotel. I was anxious to do a ride-along with Joshua and Pham. Simone wasn't interested in heading out to see alligators and Mark said he and Sarge would stay with her at the Marriott. I think she was still not a hundred percent and needed to rest more.

We headed south out of New Orleans looking to check out Gatorland--USA, supposedly the largest alligator farm in America. Their advertisements said they had more than a thousand gators at the farm and another thousand out in the swamp lands. They had several tours daily, both fast airboats and slower barges that cruised through the swamp to show you 'the biggest, meanest gators in the world.' They also had domesticated gators, raised from eggs in the gator hatchery. The biggest draw were the wild gators. Some of them were huge, over fifteen feet long, weighing more than a thousand pounds. Personally, I thought a lot of their advertisements were extremely exaggerated. When I first saw one of the big ones I changed my mind, they were enormous monsters.

We signed up for the last barge tour of the day. It was a thirty-minute ride through the swamp 'guaranteed to show you some of the nastiest animals that ever walked the Earth.' About a dozen people boarded the barge which could have easily held twice that number. I figured since it was getting dark, most people wouldn't enjoy riding through a gator infested swamp. Joshua and Pham stood next to the railing as the barge headed out into the swamp. It was getting dark and the barge pilot turned on several spot lights illuminating the area surrounding the barge. A recorded message began to play.

"Welcome ladies and gentlemen, boys and girls. Remember to keep your hands and feet well inside the barge, it's getting close to feeding time for the gators and they'd like a little variety in their meals."

The recording ended and Joshua asked the barge pilot how much the gators ate. "Well, that depends on how big they are and when they had their last meal. The big ones could easily eat a good-sized man but then they wouldn't need to eat again for a day or two."

Pham asked, "What do you feed them?"

The pilot replied, "These are wild beasts in their natural habitat. We don't feed them anything."

Joshua asked, "Have you ever had a barge sink during a tour?"

The pilot did a quick look around to see if anyone was listening to their conversation. He lowered his voice and answered, "About four or five years ago, a new pilot hit a partially submerged log and capsized his barge. The barge was loaded with tourists and they all went into the swamp." He paused and waited for a passenger to move out of ear shot before continuing, "Have you ever heard of sharks getting into a feeding frenzy?"

Joshua nodded. "Well," said the pilot, "gators, hungry gators, would put a bunch of sharks to shame. They never found any of the passengers from the capsized barge, only a few body parts. That put a real crimp in our business."

The barge bumped into something and a woman screamed. "Oh my God! Look at the size of that thing." The spot light shone brightly on the head of a huge gator as he attempted to climb onto the barge. Several others began yelling and screaming but the pilot turned the barge abruptly and the gator slipped off the bow and sunk back into the swamp. The pilot said, "Okay folks, the tour is over for tonight. We're on our way back to the dock." He laughed and added, "I hope you enjoyed your ride."

As the barge began docking, Joshua asked me, *Did you enjoy your boat trip, Caleb?*

To be honest, Josh, if I'd had a body, I would have shit myself. Why did you come out here? I thought this was supposed to be a joy ride not a horror show.

I just wanted to determine if feeding the cartel bosses to the gators was a way of getting rid of the bodies. I think I got my answer.

The ride back to the city was uneventful. As we approached the New Orleans city limits I started getting a strange feeling. I'd felt it before. It was a disturbance in the force. The closer we got, the stronger the feeling. I thought to myself, *It couldn't be Carlos, could it?* His spirit should have vanished when Manuel died. Maybe it's another evil spirit, unrelated to what was going on with us. That had to be it. New Orleans was a big city and well known for its voodoo. It's probably some voodoo witch conjuring up the spirt of some evil dead guy. Nothing to worry about. Then why was I still worrying?

We dropped off the War Wagon at the secure site. I noticed Joshua activating the wagon's security system. I didn't remember him doing that before. I wondered if he was sensing something was off.

It took us about an hour to get back to the Marriott. The city crews had done a pretty good job of cleaning up Canal Street from the explosion debris but they hadn't opened it up yet for normal traffic. There was another parade going through the French Quarter which caused us further delays. It was almost 2200 hours before we got to our suite.

When Joshua opened the door to the suite, the first thing we heard were the sounds of Simone wailing and Sarge howling.

"What's going on?" asked Joshua as he headed towards the bedroom to check on Simone.

"She's having nightmares," answered Mark. "She's been having them off and on since you left. She's been up a few times to use the bathroom and get a drink of water then she went back to sleep. I asked her what was going on and she said she can't stop thinking about Manuel and Carlos, about the way they died."

"What about Sarge?" asked Pham. "Is he having nightmares too?"

"Not sure," replied Mark. "He's never acted like this before. He hasn't been asleep so I don't think he's having nightmares. It's probably sympathy howling."

Joshua was sitting on the edge of the bed holding on to Simone's hand. She was awake, talking with him as he tried to comfort her. Sarge had stopped howling and when Joshua came in he jumped down off the bed and joined Mark in the living room. He laid on the couch next to Mark and promptly went to sleep. He was probably tired; Mark said he never sleeps when he's on guard duty.

A few minutes passed and Simone drifted off to sleep again. Joshua turned out the light, took off his shoes and laid down next to Simone, holding her in his arms. She seemed peaceful.

It had been a long day. Pham and Mark turned out the remaining lights and headed to their bedroom. Sarge remained on the couch, facing the front door. A few minutes later the suite was filled with soft snoring sounds.

It was time for me to do some recon.

Searching for a Spirit—Caleb

When Joshua goes to sleep, it's as if we're temporarily no longer bonded. I am free to roam the spirit world. Things are very different then. I no longer see or hear but I can sense the presence of other spirits. This is difficult to explain. It's not as if everyone who has passed away has a spirit roaming around in the ether. In reality, my reality, I can sense only a few spirits. Sometimes I'm not aware of any spirts. But when I sense a spirit nearby, it has a unique signature.

There also seems to be a limit on the power of spirits. When I was first bonded to Joshua, every contact I made with other humans was through him. If Joshua could see or hear a particular human I could read their thoughts. Later, through no special effort of my own, I was able to read the human's thoughts, even when Joshua couldn't see or hear them. It seemed like the longer I was bonded with Joshua my abilities continued to expand.

Contacting other spirits is a whole new ball game. Ever since I bonded with Joshua, I've been aware of other spirits but never interacted with them until Carlos came along. It was much harder to 'read' his thoughts compared to reading a human. After he was bonded to Manuel it became a little easier to mind read him but he could also block me from getting a complete data dump. He got better at blocking me after his relationship with Manuel became stronger.

Tonight I wanted to accomplish two things: first, I wanted to determine if Carlos was still floating around in the ether somewhere or did he vanish when Manuel died? Secondly, if he is still around, how strong is he and what is his purpose for existing?

As a starting point, my consciousness searched for the 'disturbance in the force' that I had come to associate with Carlos. At first there was nothing. For what seemed like a long time there was still nothing but when I'm not bonded to Joshua, time has little meaning. Gradually, I detected … something. I slowly moved in the direction of the disturbance. I could feel it grow and as it grew I could see more detail to the disturbance. After another eternity (or perhaps five minutes) I was pretty sure it was Carlos. I had a hard time believing he still existed. For some reason, I believed a spirit could only bond once and once their human passed, he ceased to exist. If it truly was Carlos my belief system was totally obsolete. I had to find out for sure.

Hello Carlos, What's up? I waited for what seemed like a really long time without any response. I tried again. *So it looks like there's going to be Mexican running your cartel soon. What a shame.*

Almost immediately I received a reply, *That will never happen.*

If I had a spine, a cold chill would have been running down it. I tried wittier dialog, however there were no further responses.

I had an answer to my first question: Carlos was still alive. I had no idea how that could possibly happen but I had to accept it and inform Joshua that Carlos was still a player.

I had no idea what Spirit Carlos was planning but we needed to find out ASAP.

DAY 10

Recovery—Simone

It was morning, early morning as best I could tell. Dim sunlight was shining through the bedroom window. I wasn't ready to get up yet so I rolled over into the arms of Joshua. He had been with me all night and it was such a comfort to have him with me, holding me, driving away my nightmares.

I must have been dozing when I heard his voice. "Time to get up. You can't sleep all day. We have things to do."

I snuggled up to him and said, "Just a few more minutes, please."

He hugged me, gently kissed my cheek, and mumbled, "What did you say?"

I hugged him back and answered, "I said I don't want to get up yet."

"Neither do I," he replied and drifted back to sleep, snoring lightly.

I awoke again, this time feeling well rested and refreshed, ready to meet the new day. Joshua was no longer next to me; I could hear the sounds of him brushing his teeth.

As I sat up on the edge of the bed, Sarge pushed the bedroom door open with his nose and peeked at me. When he saw me sitting on the bed, he walked in wagging his tail and smiling at me. He rested his snout on my knee and looked at me with his dark brown eyes.

I patted his head and told him, "I'm fine now, Sarge. Thanks for guarding me last night."

He barked once, turned and trotted back into the living room. I could hear voices and I assumed everyone was up except me. I also heard a woman's voice. I still had my Harrah's uniform on I had been wearing when I was kidnapped, it looked a mess, but the smell of food and freshly brewed coffee pulled me out of the bedroom like a giant magnet. I walked into the living room with Joshua right behind me.

Mark looked up from a plate of delicious smelling food and said, "Good morning, Simone. I trust you slept well."

I nodded and sat down next to him as an attractive woman, wearing a Marriott's uniform, placed a heaping plate of food in front of me. I began salivating at once, it had been more than a day since I had eaten anything.

"Simone, this is Trish," said Mark. "She brings us our breakfast every morning. Sarge says it's the best food he's ever eaten and he never wants to eat kibble again."

Sarge barked twice in agreement as the rest of the crew sat down to eat. I smiled at Trish as I breathed in the aroma of the meal. After the first bite I said to her, "Sarge is right. This is wonderful. It sure beats the hell out of kibble."

Trish laughed, along with the men and said, "I'm so glad you like it. Does everyone have everything you need?"

Everyone nodded their head, their mouths too full of food to speak. Trish turned to go and said, "See you all tomorrow morning. Goodbye Sarge."

Pham looked at Joshua, swallowed a fork full of egg and asked Joshua, "What's on the schedule for today, boss?"

Before he could answer, we heard the beep from his dedicated CI phone. He looked at the message, then excused himself. "I need to take this."

He stood, left the table and went into our bedroom and closed the door behind him. The rest of us continued to eat our breakfast.

Briefing on Last Night's Activities—Caleb

Joshua sat down in one of the bedroom chairs, closed his eyes and thought to me, *Good morning, Caleb, what have you got for me?*

Some good news and maybe some not-so-good news."

Give me the good news first.

I finally was able to connect with the El Mayo's IT guys last night. I found out they are putting together some kind of extravaganza for the party the evening before Mardi Gras. I don't have all the details yet but it involves avatars, lots of avatars. I think they are creating life-like figures of famous entertainers.

What kind of entertainers?"

All kinds: rock groups, movie actors, famous people from history and one particularly unsettling character.

And who would that be?

The IT people think in code, not names. For example they were making avatars they called bugs and rocks and famous actors in sex scenes 1 and 2. The only one they referred to by name was Carlos.

Joshua sat up quickly and opened his eyes. *What did they say about Carlos?*

It was all very confusing but they mentioned the traits they wanted to work into the Carlos avatar, like supernatural evil stuff; voodoo, magic and witches, souls being destroyed, that kind of stuff.

Any idea why they would use his image for a party?"

None, I replied. *I intend to keep checking the IT people to see if I can get more details about what's going on. Are you ready for the bad news?*

Joshua grimaced, then said, *Not really but go ahead. Lay it on me.*

Carlos' spirit may not have been destroyed when Manuel died.

Jacob came out of his chair and yelled, "What?!!! That isn't possible…You told m…"

Take it easy, Jacob. You're talking out loud, yelling actually. Sit back down and calm yourself.

He sat and took several deep breaths, closed his eyes, then thought, *Sorry, Caleb. Please continue.*

I think Carlos' spirit may still exist. If he does, he's a lot weaker than he was when he was bonded to Manuel. He's not bonded to anyone now. I'm sure of that.

Joshua's eyes popped open and a look of terror filled his face. *He's going after Simone. She's his daughter, the only other living relative he has. He wants to bond with her to increase his power, his ability to manipulate people. We can't let that happen!*

I got this, bro. This is going to be a spirit war and only spirits can play. I'm a lot more advanced then him. He's starting over again. You need to sit this one out and let me do my job. You take care of El Mayo and the cartels while I keep Simone clean of her evil father. You got me!

Joshua nodded his head. *I got you. And thanks.*

Debrief of the Crew—Joshua

Everyone was sitting around the table when I came out of the bedroom. I took my seat and was all business. "We have more details now of El Mayo's plan and we continue to get additional information each day. Here's what I believe will happen on the last day of Mardi Gras. The meeting will be limited to the top ten bosses of the largest cartels in the Western Hemisphere, including the Sinaloa cartel. That would bring the total to 60 people all of whom are guilty of numerous crimes including murder, drug distribution and human trafficking. Felony arrest warrants have been issued for all 60 of them, isn't that correct, Pham?"

Pham nodded. "Yes, there are an additional hundred warrants issued for many of the cartels' soldiers. Our goal is to arrest as many of these people as possible. We are to limit as many casualties to the cartel members as we can. We especially want to prevent any collateral casualties to civilians."

I moved on to the next step. "In order to comply with our mission statement, I believe we need to make these arrests well removed from where the meeting will be taking place. Fortunately, I also believe the Sinaloa cartel wants to avoid any conflict in Harrah's meeting room. They don't want to get the police involved with any of their plans. This is what I think is the most likely scenario. Once the meeting begins in the large conference room at the top of hotel, all doors will be locked and the room will be flooded with a gas that will render all the occupants dead or unconscious. None of the actual Sinaloa cartel bosses will be in the room at the time.

In their place will be body doubles. A new piece of information suggests they might be using avatars in place of the body doubles. Either way, El Mayo and his bosses will not be in the conference room. They are actually residing in the Marriott hotel and will remain there while the meeting takes place watching the show on their iPads. They will be arrested by the DEA as soon as the gas is released.

"Once everyone is dead or unconscious, the room will be cleared of gas and the bodies of the cartel loaded onto a helicopter and taken to Gatorland—USA to be dropped in the swamp and devoured by the gators. Gatorland will be closed for the Mardi Gras holiday and we will ensure there are no civilians anywhere near it.

"We expect the soldiers from the various cartels will be monitoring all of this and will follow the helicopter out to Gatorland to rescue their respective people. This will be the most likely place for armed conflict. To avoid this we will have a number of crop duster aircraft loaded with sleeping gas to put the soldiers to sleep before a battle can begin. The gas will remain effective for at least an hour and we doubt anyone will be wearing gas masks."

Everyone sat quietly for a moment, then Mark asked, "How certain are you this plan will work?"

Joshua answered, "I think there is an excellent chance no civilians will be injured. There's a 75% probability none of the cartel soldiers will be killed. The highest death rate will be of the bosses on the helicopter. They might be killed in the conference room. I doubt it but it could happen. If they aren't dead from the gas, there's only a 50% survival probability. As of now, we don't have a good method to get the helicopter to land before they dump the bosses into the swamp to become gator lunch. Of course, we could shoot it down but then everyone would probably be killed in the crash.

"If you have any reservations about the plan, let me know. I need to brief the DEA and FBI later this afternoon."

Briefing the Feds—Simone

The meeting had been set up a couple of days ago but I called to confirm everyone was going to still be present for the briefing. New Orleans PD weren't going to be able to supply many troops for the actual mission on Mardi Gras. Most of them were going to be tied up in crowd control and handling the increase in crimes that always occurred during the last day of Mardi Gras celebration. There were going to be at least five parades that day beginning at nine in the morning with the last one winding up around midnight. One bright spot was that NOLA PD SWAT would be available to support us.

I was busy coordinating some existing issues between the DEA and FBI when I thought I heard someone call my name. I didn't recognize the voice nor did I see anyone looking to speak to me. It must have been my imagination.

Joshua, better known as Isaiah Jones to the DEA and FBI, gave an expanded briefing, going into a lot more detail of the roles the federal agents would play in rounding up and arresting the soldiers from the various cartels. "I shouldn't have to tell you how dangerous these men and women are. They will not hesitate to kill anyone who gets in their way, so protect yourselves at all times. Don't wait for them to fire first. If they begin to raise a weapon at you, shoot first and keep shooting until they're down. Hopefully, the majority of these criminals will be incapacitated by the sleeping gas. It should take effect after being exposed within a couple of minutes. Keep your gas masks on at all times until the all clear has been sounded. If you don't, you may be joining them for sleepy time."

There were a number of questions from the feds and few from the SWAT teams. Maps were handed out to everyone involved showing the anticipated battle ground near the alligator farm. The locations where the various agents were to be staged were shown. The feds and SWAT teams were to wait at these staging areas until the attack signal was given.

When the briefing was finished, I took a few moments to contact my DEA boss and make sure he was happy with me in my new assignment supporting Isaiah and his crew. Several of the feds were speaking with the crew members when someone behind me said, *Are you sure you want to be part of this Carmelita. It's going to be very dangerous.*

I turned quickly to see who was speaking but there was no one behind me. I looked to see if anyone was looking at me but everybody was involved in their own conversations. A cold chill ran through my body. When Manuel helped me escape from his mother, the first thing he did when I got to New Orleans was to change my name. Now, everyone knows me as Simone, Simone Cantrell. My real name was Carmen Hernandez but only my father called me Carmelita. My father was Carlos, but he was dead killed in the helicopter explosion … *wasn't he?*

Simone Has a Problem—Caleb

Joshua, listen up. I need your full attention. It appears the spirit of Carlos is not dead. He's attempted to contact Simone at least twice since Manuel was killed. He hasn't bonded with her, at least not yet, however she starting to think she's losing her mind.

I waited for Joshua to explode but nothing happened. I began to wonder if some way he was blocked from 'hearing' what I had just thought at him. I was considering repeating myself when he replied, *This is getting to be a never-ending problem. Why isn't he dead? I don't mean mostly dead, why isn't he completely dead?*

I considered his question, then answered, *The only thing I can think of is that he had two children. After the first one died, he thinks he can bond with the second one.*

Can he do that? Can you stop him?

I'm trying, Josh. This is all new…

"*Try harder. We don't have time to deal with this. We have to give our full attention to stopping the Sinaloa cartel. Isn't there something you can do? Try thinking outside the box?*

I could feel his frustration. I was frustrated too and let it show when I answered, *This whole thing, my very existence is outside the box! Okay, you pay attention to the cartel and I'll deal with Carlos. One thing you might consider, at least as a last resort, is to come clean with Simone. Tell her the truth about me and Carlos.*

Maybe, he thought to me, *but not before the Sinaloa mission is finished.*

Taking Care of the Details—Joshua

While Caleb left to deal with Carlos, Pham, Mark and I were busy making sure all the details were taken care of. We took Sarge with us in the War Wagon and headed out to the battlefield. Our first stop was at the crop duster airstrip where Manuel had taken off in his helicopter.

There were a number of aircraft, both fixed wing and rotary, tied down next to a very dilapidated hanger. It was late afternoon and most of the aircrafts were done spraying for the day. I understood most of their flights were done in the morning when the winds were still, just to make sure what they were spraying (fertilizer, insecticides, etc.) didn't get blown over nearby residential areas. Mardi Gras took place in late winter to early spring, well before crops were planted. Until the crops were planted there wasn't much need to do any spraying. The aircraft mechanics used this time to service the aircraft and their spraying equipment. The pilots used the time to practice their flying. It takes tremendous skill to fly an aircraft low and slow over their target fields and still avoid flying into power lines or over highways with heavy traffic. They have to make sure their spray covers the entire field without over spraying adjacent fields.

When crop dusting was in its infancy, there weren't any aircrafts designed to dust crops. Instead, mechanics had to modify the planes by adding spray bars, storage tanks and controls to turn the spray on and off. That led to wide variety of configurations, some more effective than others.

The choice of aircrafts used for spraying also varied. Usually, old biplanes were preferred. They could carry sufficient spray and were the best for flying low and slow. There were a lot of them available and they were relatively cheap. All the biplanes had open cockpits which resulted in the pilots being covered in spray. That could be a problem when they start spraying sleeping gas, even with the pilots wearing gas masks.

I watched as Mark turned Sarge loose to chase whatever he could find. Apparently, he must have found quite a few critters from the looks of him streaking through the high grass.

I was standing in front of the open hanger when I heard a voice behind me. "Are you interested in that Stearman? I can make you a real good deal. It's in pristine condition. And by the way that is one fine ride you got there," he added as he checked out the wagon.

I turned to look at a man in his late sixties walking out of the hanger. He was wearing a flight suit covered in grease and grime and using a rag to wipe some of it off his hands and arms. "You interested in buying?" he asked again. "By the way, call me Norm."

"Well Norm, my name is Isaiah and I'm not interested in buying, I'm looking for crop dusters to do some spraying," I answered.

"I can help you there too, Isaiah. Where do you want to dust and what kind of juice are you planning on using?"

"I need some dusting done over by the big field just north of Gatorland. I need to get rid of some … pests. These pests are nasty and we'll need to use some pretty strong juice to take them all out. The duster pilots will have to wear gas masks."

Norm took a minute to check me out. "You aren't military, are you? Your ride is impressive but it doesn't look military."

"Used to be. How about you?"

"Air Force. Retired Chief Master Sargent. Aircraft mechanic." He paused for a minute then asked, "If I read you right, you must be a fed. And if you're a fed, none of my pilots can handle what you have in mind."

He started to turn away, then turned back and added, "I may have some information you'd be interested in. Are you familiar with the C-130?"

I nodded. "Yes chief, I had the pleasure of flying on one a few months ago with some Marines."

He reached up and scratched his head, like he was trying to decide if he should tell me something. "Well a year or so ago, when the big hurricane came through here, the land you're talking about was flooded waste deep. That led to a bug infestation like I have never seen before or after. The Air Force sent four specially equipped C-130s down here to spray them bugs. They were the only Air Force planes to ever be equipped with the Modular Aerial Spray System. It was the damnedest thing I'd ever seen. Four of those transports came flying over my place here in an echelon right formation with flaps and gear down, right on the edge of stalling out, spraying some of the nastiest juice I've ever had the displeasure to inhale. They did it three days in a row and no more bugs."

"Is that so, Norm? Well, you've really got my attention. Do you know where those C-130s are based?"

"While they were spraying here they were temporarily based at Barksdale AFB, in Louisiana. I think their home base was the Youngstown Air Reserve Station in Ohio."

"Norm, you have made my day. I cannot thank you enough but I'll be back to show my appreciation," I said as I handed him one of my business cards.

"You could buy the Stearman, I'd appreciate that," he said with a straight face, then broke out laughing. As he turned to head back into the hanger, he said, "Good hunting, Isaiah. Hope you can get rid of those pesky bugs."

I rounded up Mark and Sarge and met Pham at the War Wagon to head back to New Orleans. Sarge was plum tuckered out from chasing the critters and he and Mark sat in the back, resting. I asked Pham to drive and I took the front passenger seat and called my handler.

"Boss, I have a request." I filled him in over the encrypted phone and he said he would have everything waiting for us at Barksdale AFB the day before Mardi Gras, complete with the sleeping gas I wanted.

After I hung up, I was able to relax during the rest of the ride home. It was great to finally catch a break.

A Long Day—Simone

I feel exhausted. It seemed like this day would never end. Now that it is almost over, I'm a little afraid of going to sleep. It seems like I'm starting to hear voices when there's nobody there. That can't be good. I need to talk to somebody about the voices but I'm not sure who to talk to. What would Joshua say if I told him I was hearing voices. Would he think I'm going nuts? Worse than that, how could I explain to him I think the voices are really just one voice, the voice of my dead father. Joshua is way too busy with the cartel mission to listen to the babbling of a silly woman. I need to toughen up and not let the minor traumas in my life overwhelm me! I'm going to sleep.

<u>DAY 11</u>

<u>Attempting to Bond with My Daughter—Carlos</u>

I waited until she was sound asleep before I began. Then, in my most soothing voice, barely a whisper, I entered her mind, *Carmelita, it's your papi.*

I waited and watched her reaction. She didn't move, her breathing remained the same. After a moment, I repeated, this time a little louder, *Carmelita, it's your papi.*

Her body flinched and there was a brief pause in her breathing as she rolled over. Perfect! I had contacted her on a subconscious level. Time to go to work.

Mija, please listen to me. What I have to tell you is very important. This isn't a dream, it's a vision. I am dead now, killed by a man you think loves you. I am looking down on you from heaven and I have a message for you. Don't believe Joshua, he is a liar controlled by the devil and he will kill you just like he killed me and your brother. You must protect yourself from him and his friends. You must kill them all. If you don't, they will kill you! Remember this vision, mija. You must kill them all.

As I was delivering my message, she became agitated, her breathing ragged but she remained asleep. When I was done planting my instructions I stopped and waited for her to drift back into a deeper sleep, then I waited ten minutes more and repeated my vision. I did this three times during the night. She awoke after the last time and staggered into

the bathroom. When she returned, she fell into her bed
sobbing quietly.

It Was Going to be a Good Day—Joshua

We arrived late from our trip to locate crop dusters. Norm's suggestion to use the C-130s was a Godsend and I was very pumped up. Simone had gone to bed before we returned and I checked to make sure she was all right. When I saw she was sleeping peacefully, I closed the bedroom door quietly and decided to sleep on the couch. Sarge decided there wasn't enough room for the two of us; he jumped down and headed for the other bedroom.

When morning came, I was awakened by the sound of the shower. I waited for Simone to finish but after what I considered a long time, she hadn't come out of the bedroom to join us.

After Pham, Mark and Sarge had come out of their bedroom, I used their bathroom. When I had finished my business, minus my shower, the others decided to go for their morning run before breakfast. They invited me to join them but I said I wanted to take a shower. Actually, I was beginning to worry about Simone.

Is Simone all right? I thought to Caleb.

Not sure, he answered, *I'm having a tough time reading her.*

What?!! I exclaimed.

Something's trying to block me form accessing her. I'm only getting partial info. I sense Carlos is involved, he replied.

Why didn't you tell me sooner?

You told me to handle it. I'm handling it. Carlos hasn't bonded with her, at least not yet. However, he's trying to block me as well. It's like listening to a conversation and hearing every other word.

I decided. *I'm going in.*

I knocked twice on the bedroom door. "Simone can I come in? I need to take a shower."

When she didn't answer, I opened the door and saw her sitting on the edge of the bed. Her eyes were closed and she seemed to be mumbling something I couldn't hear. She was holding her Glock in both hands, aiming it at the floor.

"GUN!!!"

I wasn't sure if it was me or Caleb who shouted out the warning or maybe we both did.

I moved very slowly toward her, sat down on the bed next to her and leaned close to hear what she was mumbling.

"…kill them all before they kill me…Have to kill them all before they kill me…Have to kill…"

She opened her eyes and smiled at me. It was a sad smile. The gun came up slowly. I reached over and took it from her, clicked on the safety, ejected the round from the chamber and removed the magazine. Then I started to breathe again.

Caleb was speechless a first, if I remembered correctly.

Simone sagged against me and began sobbing. I put my arm around her and held her tightly. Between sobs, she said, "I'm so sorry *papi*, I can't do it. I can't kill any of them. Please forgive me. I'm too weak."

Then she screamed, a very long, loud scream and passed out, falling back onto the bed.

I checked her pulse, it was racing and she began to tremble and shake.

She's having a seizure! Call 911, Caleb was screaming at me. *Hurry, Josh. She can't die. Please God, don't let her die!*

It took the EMTs five minutes to arrive and another five to stabilize her. She was going to be all right, they assured me. The rest of the team showed up from their run as the EMTs were leaving. I told them the same thing they told me. "She had a psychotic break probably caused by the physical and mental trauma of the kidnapping and the loss of her father and brother." If they only knew the truth, they'd be as freaked out as I was.

She was barely conscious as Sarge jumped up on the bed and joined her, gently licking her hand. Her eyes were barely open as she began petting him before drifting off into a medically induced sleep.

I tried to contact Caleb but he wasn't responding. I had the idea he might be searching for Carlos.

Trish knocked on the door and brought in our breakfast. Nobody was hungry except possibly Sarge. He came out of the bedroom, smelled his plate of food, licked Trish's hand as his thank you, took one piece of bacon and went back to comfort Simone.

This wasn't the way I had thought today was going to start.

The Hunt for Carlos—Caleb

I was going to kill him. I didn't care what it was going to cost me. That spirit was going to die. I prayed I was the spirit who was going to end his miserable existence. He had caused more pain and suffering than any man I know. He was right up there with Hitler, Stalin and Pol Pot. How could such a soulless creature ever exist, especially exist beyond the death of the body? I didn't want him just dead, I wanted him to suffer the pain of a thousand deaths.

I remembered my father, Papa Moses, telling us what the Bible said about the fate of the wicked at the end of time, "In the book of Revelation it says the wicked will be thrown into the lake of fire to be burned forever and ever."

I desperately wanted to be the one to throw Carlos into that lake of fire and sit on the shore and watch him burn forever and ever. As I pictured that, another verse from the Bible occurred to me, "Vengeance is mine, sayeth the Lord."

For some reason, remembering that verse had a calming effect on me. Slowly, very slowly, the anger left me. What remained was the determination I wouldn't permit Carlos to hurt anymore people, so help me God.

Next Steps—Joshua

Once we were positive Simone was resting quietly, we all decided to try to finish the breakfast Trish left for us. We weren't particularly hungry but there's an old Marine saying: "Sleep and eat whenever you can. You may not get another chance for a long time."

Pham heated our meals in our microwave. When Sarge smelled the food, he turned from Simone and began eating from his plate left on the floor. It didn't seem to matter to him that the food was cold. He finished eating and returned to be with Simone.

The three of us talked while we ate. Mark was the first to speak up. "I think we need to get Simone professional help. Right now I see her as a danger to herself, all of us and the mission."

Pham shrugged his shoulders as he took another bite, indicating he wasn't sure. I disagreed.

"I went through the same thing when my twin brother died in Kabul. I knew he was dead but I kept hearing him, like he was right beside me or inside my head. I was in a hospital for a year living on happy pills and psychoanalysis."

"Did it help?" Pham asked.

"Not at all. In fact it made it worse."

"How did you get better? You seem pretty squared away to me," said Mark.

"Thanks," I replied. "Once I got the meds out of my system and could think clearly again, I gradually got better. It was up and down for a long time. I'd go days without hearing my brother's voice, then he'd show up and talk my ear off for a couple of days before disappearing again."

"Did you ever actually see him? I mean like a hallucination?" Pham questioned.

"No, not really. Once, in the beginning I looked in the mirror and thought I was looking at him but it was just my reflection."

Pham looked like he wasn't sure if he should ask but decided to ask the question I get asked a lot who know about my condition. "Do you still hear him?"

"Every day," I answered and got the same look of surprise everyone has when they ask that question.

"But I've learned to live with it," I continued. "In a way, it's kind of comforting. It's like he's not really dead. I mean, I know he's dead but hearing him in my head gives me a peace of mind. Does any of this make any sense to you? I usually don't share this type of information. I hope you will keep it to yourselves."

They both nodded, then Mark asked, "What do we do about Simone? Once we come down to the short strokes on the mission we won't be able to protect her."

"I know but for right now, let's take it day by day. Is that all right with both of you?"

They nodded their agreement and I heard Sarge bark his agreement through the open bedroom door.

Filling in the Blanks—Caleb

When I contacted Joshua, he asked me to help him fill in more detail regarding our cartel neighbors. He wanted to know the room numbers of each of the bosses and what would be their probable location when the action goes down on Mardi Gras at Harrah's.

Since I was sure Simone was being protected and it was unlikely Carlos could override the sleeping potion the EMTs had given her, I figured I had at least an hour to do my voodoo.

It was really pretty straight forward to read a few minds and get all the info I needed. I sent the room numbers of all the bosses and their probable location when the Sinaloa dropped the hammer on the other cartels.

It turns out they all plan to meet in a small conference room in the Marriott on the main floor. They get to watch the show live on an 80-inch flat paneled television. Snacks and drinks will be provided.

The DEA will be waiting in the hallway for them after the show is over.

I transmitted this information to the printer in our suite so Joshua could have documentation to share with our partners

Before I moved on to my next assignment, I checked with Joshua on Simone's status. He told me she was still sedated but resting comfortably. He then asked me if I'd like to go on a scouting trip. I said 'you bet' and transferred myself in the twinkling of an eye to be bonded to him.

Fly Me To the Moon—Joshua

Since the other guys weren't joining us, we took the rental instead of the War Wagon and headed out to go for a plane ride.

When we arrived at the crop duster's small dirt runway, Norm greeted me as I got out of the car. The first thing he said was, "Hi Isaiah. What happened to your souped-up ride?"

"Keeping a low profile today."

"Good enough. Are you ready to cheat death?"

"Sure am, Norm."

Wait! thought Caleb. *What's this about cheating death? I don't want to be cheating death, just a nice comfortable ride in a late model airplane.*

Not happening, bro. We're taking the Stearman.

Oh my God! That's not an airplane, that's a century old relic.

That's why we're going to be cheating death, I said as I walked over to the airplane and climbed into the front cockpit, actually just a hole in the top of the fuselage, aft of the overhead wing. I sat down on a flat board that doubled as a seat and strapped in.

Norm yelled up at me, "The starter motor is out. I'm going to have to prop it."

I feel like I'm trapped in the 1930s. Come on, what kind of an engine has to be propped? asked Caleb.

The kind that don't have a starter motor. It'll only take a few minutes, I replied.

Norm stood in front and a little off to one side and yelled, "Chalks in place."

"Roger, chalks in place."

"Mags off."

"Roger, mags off," I said as I turned the magneto switch to the off position.

"Throttle setting to one-quarter."

"Roger, throttle setting on one-quarter," I said as I moved the throttle setting to the one-quarter position.

"Mixture setting to rich."

"Roger, mixture setting to rich," I said as I pushed the mixture lever to max.

"Walking it through," said Norm as he grabbed the tip of the propeller and pulled the propeller through two complete revolutions.

Then we went through it again but this time the magnetos were turned on and when Norm pulled the prop very quickly the engine began chugging away. I placed my feet on the two rudder pedals and pushed down locking the brakes, keeping the Stearman from moving.

Norm quickly pulled the two chalks from the wheels, ran to the side of the plane and climbed into the rear cockpit hole. The noise of the radial engine was deafening until Norm signaled me to put on a headset.

The headset muffled the noise and allowed me to talk back and forth with Norm. The first thing he said to me was, "I've got the airplane. Take your hands and feet off the controls and don't touch anything. Where do you want to go?"

"I want to follow the river. I'm looking for places where there's heavy growth along the shore line."

As Norm banked the biplane to the left and headed towards the Mississippi, I thought toward Caleb, *How're you liking your plane ride so far?*

I waited but there was no reply. *Caleb, are you still with me?* Still no answer. I figured flying in a noisy, opened cockpit relic of an airplane wasn't to his liking. He must have decided to do something else.

When we reached the river, Norm banked right and began following it as it meandered through southern Louisiana on its way to the gulf. There was a lot of shoreline with dense growth which would offer excellent cover for our federal agents to hide from the cartel soldiers. The river also provided a stealthy passage way to deliver the feds way before the C-130s began putting the cartel soldiers to sleep. I took numerous pictures which I would use to decide which were the best hiding spots.

Simone Under Attack Again—Caleb

I left Norm and Joshua to their fun and games when I sensed Carlos was at it again. One of the really neat features of being a spirit is, it takes no time at all to travel. One moment I'm riding along with Joshua in the ancient aircraft, laughingly known as a Stearman PT 13. Rumor had it the plane was built about the time dinosaurs roamed the Earth. The next instant, I'm face-to-face with Carlos. Well, not really, that's just an expression.

I sensed he was badgering Simone again and I planned to put a stop to it. He must have been waiting for her to wake up from the sleeping potion the med tech had given her. Now that she was awake, Carlos was firing both barrels at her. *Why didn't you shoot them when you had the chance? You could have killed all of them. They were all together in one room. What is wrong with you? Why can't you follow a simple order. Who knows when you will get anoth…*

Simone cut him off, screaming at the top of her lungs while Mark and Sarge watched helplessly. To them it appeared she was yelling at some imaginary person threatening her. "STOP!!! Get out of my head. You're dead, you're not real, you're driving me CRAZY"

She's right, Carlos. I projected at him. Leave her alone. She's already made her choice and you lose. Why don't you go off into a corner and cease to exist? You're in such a hurry to kill somebody, why don't you kill yourself?

Carlos screamed in frustration with me interrupting, then projected, *Stop him. Silence him so he can't interrupt me. I must have a clear path to her if I'm going to be successful.*

Several things happened at once. I was positive Simone couldn't have heard the thoughts I had aimed at Carlos. Obviously, Carlos' last comments weren't aimed at me or Simone. She was looking around the room with wild eyes but didn't seem to have heard her father's last words.

I realized there was another player in the room but I couldn't sense the new spirit at all.

The next thing I knew, I was no longer in the room. I couldn't sense anything. *Had Carlos continued his tirade with Simone?*

I couldn't tell. Whoever, the new spirit was he had shut me down completely. I couldn't even sense Joshua. Was this the end of me? It felt like it could be.

<u>**Where's Caleb? —Joshua**</u>

When I got back to the Marriott, I expected Caleb would be there but he wasn't. I tried to contact him on the elevator ride to our floor but he didn't reply. He always replied to me immediately when I called him but not this time. When I walked into our suite, I was met by two EMTs on their way out. Mark and Pham didn't look happy. "What's going on? Why are the EMTs here again? Is Simone okay?" I asked as I walked towards the closed bedroom door.

I opened the door and saw Simone lying on the bed wearing restraints on her hands and legs. "What the hell?"

Mark said, "You need to sit down with us, boss."

I sat down on the couch next to Sarge. Before he could continue I noticed the bruising on his face and arms. "Are you okay? What happened, Mark? Did the cartel…"

Mark raised his hand to silence me and I shut up and waited for him to tell me what had happened. "Sarge barked once to let me know Simone was waking up from the sedative. We kept the bedroom door opened so we could look in on her from time to time. She sat on the edge of the bed for a while with her arm around Sarge. After a few minutes she headed for the bathroom. Pham went into our bedroom to check on the data we were getting from the bugs in the penthouse suites and the conference rooms. When Simone came out of the bathroom she smiled and waved at me before she sat down next to Sarge again. She was humming a song and was acting normal. That lasted about ten minutes before she went off again. She went from being completely normal to a full outrage in about five seconds. She was screaming, like she was screaming at somebody in the room but other than her and Sarge, the room was empty."

"Do you remember what she was saying?" I asked, looking for some clue as to what set her off again.

Mark nodded, and replied, "She kept saying pretty much the same things over and over—Leave me alone, get out of my head, I'm not going to kill them—things like that. Then she stopped screaming and stood very still like she was listening to somebody. Then she started up again. I remember exactly what she said. 'I won't kill them. I'm going to kill myself instead and send you straight to hell.' At that point, I ran into the bedroom to restrain her. I didn't know if she had a weapon or not but I didn't want to risk it. When I reached out to hold on to her she used her jiujitsu on me. She pretty much beat me to a pulp. Sarge was barking at her and tried to stop her but she was incredibly fast and strong. When Pham came running in to see what was going down, she had me in a choke hold and he had to use his stun gun on her several times until she let go. I don't think she knew it was me trying to keep her from hurting herself. Pham put her back into her restraints as I called the EMT to give her another sedative."

I was stunned by what I just heard. I knew what had happened. It was Carlos again. He was trying to get her to kill us but she turned the tables on him when she said she would kill herself just to get rid of him.

I also had a really bad feeling in my gut. Somehow, Carlos was able to shut down Caleb. That's why he didn't respond to my call. I was praying it was only a temporary situation and not permanent. I don't know what I would do if I didn't have my brother with me.

Oblivion—Caleb

The good news was I wasn't dead. I was still a functioning spirit. The bad news was I was very much alone and unable to make any type of contact with anyone, not Joshua, not any of the people from the cartel and not even Carlos. He had to have something to do with my present state. However, I had no idea how he could've done this. I know he had to have had help, he couldn't possibly have done it by himself.

In some ways, this state was worse than death. There was no concept of time. For some reason a Bible verse occurred to me. "For God, a day is like a thousand years and a thousand years is like a day." I think it was from 2nd Peter, Chapter 3 but I don't remember the number of the verse.

I was in agony. Without my bond with Joshua, I had no purpose. I began to remember things from my past. I hadn't consciously decided to take that trip down memory lane but hey, it's not like I had somewhere to be. So why not relive my life as well as my spirit life.

The memories flooded into my consciousness, beginning with my earliest memories as a baby. I was surprised by the detail of my memories. As they continued, I had the feeling I wasn't just remembering these events, I was reliving them in the minutest detail. It wasn't like watching some Netflix extravaganza. It was more than sights and sounds, it was feelings too.

When I saw myself as a child and a bully smacked me in the mouth, there were a kaleidoscope of feelings, the pain in my mouth from the hit, the taste of blood as I pulled out the broken tooth (a baby tooth as I remember). I also felt the embarrassment of getting hit, then the rage that burned inside me as I attempted to defend myself. Jacob was there with me and the two of us took care of that bully. I remembered how sore my skinned knuckles felt after I had returned fire. Mostly, I felt the love for my brother for coming to my aid.

It went on and on like that, reliving everything in my life and I began feeling the dread building in me. I knew my death was coming and I really didn't want to relive that event but I had no control.

I was on a recon sweep of the northern part of Kabul. I was in enemy territory along with my platoon. Joshua wasn't with me, he had been relieved of duty for this mission and was on the other side of the city when it happened. The Taliban controlled the neighborhood we were scouting and they blended in with the locals, many of whom were Taliban supporters. I noticed a man standing on the street corner across from me. He was talking on the phone as he waved to me. I waved back, then noticed he wasn't waving, he was flipping me the bird. He was the trigger man for the IED. An instant later the bomb went off. My last memories of being alive were the incredible pain of being blown into little pieces and the sight of my right foot being ripped off my leg, then blackness, complete and total blackness that seemed to last an eternity.

At the end of that eternity, I saw a pinpoint of light shining through the blackness. As the pinpoint expanded the pain came with it, along with the screaming. I was confused, how did I survive the explosion? I knew for sure my body parts couldn't have been put back together again.

How could I possibly be alive enough to make all that screaming.

It took over a year to realize it wasn't my body that had been screaming. It wasn't me looking back at me in the mirror in the hospital bathroom. It was Joshua but how could I see Joshua? I was dead. I shouldn't be seeing anything at all.

I relived the entire year over again, one day at a time. When I finally figured out I was a spirit bonded to my twin brother, I had the unenviable task of convincing Joshua who I was. At first, he thought I was the ghost of Caleb who came back from the dead to haunt him. Eventually, we worked things out.

When he began his series of missions to help those in need of some serious help, I was in the background, giving him some hints on things to consider or how best to deal with wicked people who attempted to take him out.

During this last mission, it was very much like it was when I was alive. We communicated, joked, argued and shared ideas. We were a team again.

The story of Caleb continued right up to the point where I was floating in limbo. When my life memories ended, things went black again … and I felt myself waning. So this was truly the end.

Then I noticed a disturbance. It was very different from the negative disturbance when Carlos began executing his evil plan. This was a positive disturbance and it continued to grow. The blackness began to fade as my surroundings got lighter.

I sensed, no, not sensed, I saw as if I had eyes to see and I saw a man moving towards me. He was an old man but looked to be in great condition. He wore a white robe that reminded me of a judge's garment, except the robe judges wear are black. He reminded me of a Marine drill instructor I had the pleasure of meeting during basic training. This spirit, at least I thought it was a spirit, smiled at me (drill sergeants rarely smile) and said in the voice of an entity clearly in charge, *Hello, Master Sergeant Caleb Brown, my name is Joaquin Castelan. I'm here to assist you in getting you reinstated. Do you wish to be rebonded to your twin brother, Master Sergeant Joshua Brown?*

DAY 12

Going to Church—Joshua

I got up early on Sunday morning and searched the internet to see what churches were close to us. I settled on Vieux Carre Baptist Church on Dauphine Street in the French Quarter, only a short walk from our hotel. I was putting on the suit I'd bought in DC and had only worn it one time, for the briefing meeting with the brass.

I was dressing in the living room. I didn't want to disturb Simone but left the bedroom door opened so I could tell when she got up. Sarge was on the couch as usual, facing toward my bedroom to keep an eye on Simone.

Mark was yawning as he came out of his bedroom and walked over to Sarge to give him his morning hug. He was wearing his pajama pants with no top and his upper body and face were covered in bruises. He looked over at me and did a double take. "What's up with the fancy duds?"

"Going to church," I answered. "Service starts at 1030 hours. You and Sarge are invited to join us, Pham too."

"What about Simone?" he asked cautiously. "Who's going to watch her?"

"I am. She's going with me," I replied. "She's the main reason for me going."

Pham walked out the bedroom, dressed in his street clothes, took one look at me and let out a low whistle. "Dude, what's the occasion?"

I repeated what I had said to Mark, Pham looked at Mark who just shrugged his shoulders. Pham had a pensive expression as he asked me, "Boss, do you really think this is a good idea? I mean it's been almost 2,000 years since the Apostles were casting out demons."

"I'm not looking to have her demons cast out. I just want her to speak with a pastor. He might be able to help her. I have more faith a pastor could help more than the quacks who wanted to dope me up for the rest of my life. You're welcome to stay or go with us. It's your choice."

Simone began stirring and Sarge jumped down from the couch and up on Simone's bed, giving her hand a good-morning lick.

She smiled at him and turned and looked at me. "Don't you look all suave in your suit," she said with smile in my direction. Then she looked at Mark and her expression changed to a look of horror. "Oh my God, what happened to you, Mark?" Then her expression changed again as the memories of yesterday came back to her. "Did I do that to you?"

Mark stared at her for a moment before answering. He tried to keep his voice light and casual as he answered, "Don't worry about it, Simone. I've had worse beatings, besides, you didn't break any of my bones. I consider that a plus."

She started to cry and turned away but Pham added, "Hey, don't worry. You'll get over this. All of us have gone through similar bad times. You're one of us now, part of our team. So why don't you get up and get dressed and join us for church this morning. We can't go without you."

She stopped crying and wiped away the tears with the bed sheet. She stood up and tried to smile, it was a weak one but she was trying. "Okay teammates, give me half an hour to get dressed and put on my face."

As she closed the bedroom door Mark turned to me and asked, "What's wrong with her face. It looked fine to me. I'm the one who needs a new face. In fact, I need a whole new body."

Pham laughed and pretended to inspect Marks injuries, then said, "In the words of an old Marine buddy of mine, 'just rub some dirt on it, you'll be fine. It's a pity you won't have any scars.'"

Mark started to laugh but then winced at the pain it caused and stopped.

Trish came in with breakfast and we all ate quickly and headed off for church. Sarge joined us dressed in his best therapy dog vest.

Vieux Carre Baptist Church—Pastor Tom

As I usually do, I stood at the front doors to the church to greet our regular parishioners as well as any new guests who decided to join us. Since we were in the middle of Mardi Gras week, I didn't expect many to come to church today. The temptations of the flesh are great this time of year and many succumb to the temptation. I figured we'd be about half full today but we'd make up for it next Sunday when they returned to ask forgiveness for all the sins they committed during the festival. I sighed and thought of the Bible text that comes to mind every year around this time, 'The spirit is willing but the flesh is weak,' from the book of Matthew, Chapter 26, Verses 40 to 43.

It was almost time for the service to begin, when I spotted an unusual group coming down the sidewalk toward the church. The man in front was an extremely large black man dressed in a very expensive suit. He had to be well over six feet tall and very muscular. His hair was cut in what the military call high and tight. With him were two additional men, an attractive woman I estimated to be in her mid-twenties and a dog or perhaps it was a domesticated wolf from the size of him. One man was relatively small and of Asian descent. The other man was white. Both with high and tight haircuts and both were casually dressed as was the woman whom I think might have been of Hispanic descent.

What a combination: one black, one white, one Asian, one Hispanic and one wolf-dog wearing a therapy dog vest.

The black man in the suit approached me as our ushers closed the front doors to the lobby. The organ music had begun signaling the choir to begin singing in about five minutes.

When he spoke to me his voice was deep and strong, like the sound of distant thunder. "Pastor, my name is Isaiah Jones. Would it be possible for us to speak with you in private after the service?"

"Of course my son, I'd be happy to meet with you all. Could you tell me what you would like to talk about?

The Asian man spoke up first, "Casting out demons."

The black man turned and glared at him before continuing but I spoke first, "Well you've come to the right place. Just a few blocks from here is a voodoo priestess. If I can't help you, I'm sure she can." They all smiled at my answer. All except the woman whose face remained expressionless.

The black man, Isaiah, said, "One of our team is suffering from an extreme case of PTSD. We're wondering if you could give her some words of encouragement?"

"Of course," I said. I was about to say more but the choir began their first hymn and I ushered the group into the sanctuary. I had one of my deacons direct them to a pew where they could all sit together, including the wolf-dog.

The choir sang three hymns which was followed by *Amazing Grace* performed by a string quartet and sung by our choir director. During that special hymn, I looked at the new group and noticed they were all singing along with the choir. The woman, she had introduced herself as Simone, was sitting next to Isaiah with the wolf-dog lying at her feet. The other two men were on the other side of her.

When the music was over, one of our elders read a scripture that had to do with temptation. When he was done I stood behind the pulpit, looked at the meager turn out, smiled and began. "I'm so happy to see so many of you in attendance today." There were a few chuckles from those in the pews thinking I was being sarcastic. "I'm serious, you here today are strong in your faith. Strong enough to resist the temptations of the devil. Those who belong to our flock who didn't show up may have very good, legitimate reasons for not attending but I'm also sure there were some who gave in to temptation and may have committed sins in the process. Are we to condemn these people? Of course not. They are sinners but who isn't? The Apostle Paul said it loud and said it best: No one is righteous, no not one, for all of us are sinners."

I paused to let that sink in and listen to a few halleluiahs. I couldn't miss the halleluiah from our guest, Isaiah. I nodded at him and went on. "Since we are all sinners does that mean there is no hope for our salvation?"

There was a resounding No from Isaiah. I looked at him and asked, "Then how are we to be saved?"

Isaiah stood up and in the strong voice of a leader who knows the Bible said, "By faith in our Lord Jesus Christ our sins are forgiven and we are saved."

Everyone in the congregation was staring at him, some with opened mouths wondering who the man who speaks with such authority was. There was even a smattering of applause as he sat back down.

I continued the sermon and if I do say so myself, it was one of the best sermons I had ever preached. I considered repeating it next Sunday for those sinners who had missed this week's service.

When everyone had left the sanctuary, we met by the altar and she told me her story and what a story it was. I was fascinated by what she had gone through and how it affected her and those around her. She was honest and held nothing back. She spoke the most but the others all contributed about similar experiences but none were as heart wrenching as what this woman had gone through, was still going through. It took her almost two hours to tell it all and she was emotionally drained.

In seminary, I was taught to shut up and listen, speak only when asked a question or when you sense a contradiction in what they have said. We were also taught when a person stops sharing and it seems like they are leaving out important details, to encourage them to continue. This woman left nothing out. When she stopped talking there was nothing more for her to say.

I ended our discussion with the following comments, "Simone, thank you for trusting me enough to share what you have been going through. I am encouraged by your honesty and the willingness to risk this discussion. I want you to know, you're well on the way to solving your problems. What you have done today is called catharsis by counselors and psychologists. The word means to cleanse yourself. I also want to add, you have such great support from these three men. They have and will continue to have your back no matter what happens in the future. You need to count on them for help."

I was a little surprised when the wolf-dog growled at me, his handler, Mark I think was his name, laughed and said,

"Sarge has also been a very important part of Simone's recovery. He just wants you to acknowledge him."

With some trepidation, I reached out and gingerly pet the wolf-dog on the head. He licked my hand in return.

I closed with a prayer for her quick recovery and sent them on their way. When Simone reached the bottom step in our entryway, she turned and ran back up the steps and grabbed me in the strongest bearhug I'd ever experienced. I was concerned she might have cracked one of my ribs but to see the joy on her face was worth the pain.

"Thank you, pastor. Thank you for everything." Then she turned, ran down the steps and joined her friends.

As they walked out of sight, I turned and walked back into the church, praising God as I went.

Here Come Da Judge—Joaquin Castelan

I could see the spirit called Caleb staring at me with the expression of total shock. I need to explain. When I say I 'see' a spirit, it's not the same as one human being seeing another. It's much more complicated than that. Of course I see the image of the person the spirit represents but I also see their feelings, their emotions, their very thoughts are visible to me and can't be hidden. I know what they are going to say even before they do. Most importantly, it's impossible for them to lie to me. That's why I'm a judge.

As a judge, I must decide how to resolve conflict between spirits. In order to be unbiased in my decision making, I observe the entire life time and spirit time of all those parties who are involved in the conflict. In this case, I observed everything that ever happened to Caleb Brown. In addition, I also made a similar observation of his nemesis, Carlos Hernandez.

When the conflict between these two spirits reached a certain point, I stepped in and isolated both parties before the conflict escalated to unacceptable levels. While they were isolated, I made my observations, paying very close attention to the thoughts and actions of both parties as the conflict became more intense. I also factored in their interactions with humans during the conflict. I was ready to make my judgement.

I materialized both spirts into what appeared to them to be a small room. I gave them temporary bodies and the ability to speak. They sat in chairs and faced each other with me in the middle.

"Spirits, I was made aware of an unacceptable level of conflict between you two. I am here to resolve that conflict."

The spirit called Carlos stood and asked in an arrogant tone of voice, "Who do you think you are to interfere in my business? Why should I bother to listen to you?"

Using my calmest voice, I answered, "I'm your judge, jury and if needed, your executioner."

"Who gave you the right to tell me what to do or not do? I don't recognize your authority over me. This is just some…"

I was tired of his blustering and took away his mouth. He looked startled and stumbled backwards into his chair, running his hand over his face to see what happened to his mouth.

I turned toward Caleb and said, "This won't take long, please bear with me for a few moments.

"Carlos, I find you guilty of the following charges:

A spirit is permitted to bond with only one human. When that human dies the spirit is no longer viable and may not attempt to bond with another human—Guilty as charged.

A spirit isn't permitted to enlist the support of any advanced spirit to aid them in any form of conflict that may lead to the intentional death of a human—Guilty as charged.

A spirit isn't permitted to enlist the assistance of any angel or demon at any time—Guilty as charged.

Carlos Hernandez, you are found guilty of all three changes. Before I pronounce your sentence, I would like to make a few closing comments: You were one of the most despicable human beings who ever lived. As a spirit, you were even worse. During your existence you brought more pain, suffering and death to more people than any other person in recent memory. Therefore, I sentence you to permanent non-existence."

Caleb and I watched as the figure of Carlos Hernandez disappeared from his chair with a little pop.

I turned to look at Caleb who sat rigidly in his chair with his mouth opened, not sure he could believe what just happened.

"Now let's get you rebonded to your brother, shall we?"

"Could I ask you a couple of questions first?" he asked.

"Of course. Fire away," I replied.

"Are you an angel?"

"Absolutely not!" I replied. "I'm a spirit, just like you."

He shook his head and said, "You're nothing like me. You did things I couldn't even dream of, let alone perform."

"Perhaps, but I'm still a spirit who was given the assignment to ensure that spirits, all spirits, follow the rules or suffer the consequences. That's enough for now."

"One more question, please?"

I nodded.

"How many years have gone by since I've been here?"

"Years? It only seems like years. It's really only been a few hours. Now I really must go, I have other cases to deal with. Oh, by the way, you won't remember much of what transpired here. It's for the best. Rest assured, Carlos will not bother you or anyone else ever again. Good day to you, Caleb."

Rebonding with Joshua—Caleb

In an instant, I was inside Joshua's mind. The abruptness was startling to both of us. Joshua had been standing near the table speaking with Mark when I reappeared. His knees buckled and his speech slurred momentarily. He lost his balance and fell back into a nearby chair. Mark was at his side in an instant calling for the rest of the team to help.

Simone came running out of the bedroom to see Joshua nearly falling out of the chair as he grabbed his head with both hands. She was at his side in an instant, steading him on the chair and asked, "What the hell just happened to him?"

Mark was confused. "I don't know what happened. We were just talking about troop deployment when it looked like he was having a seizure. He stopped talking, grabbed his head and fell into the chair. Do you think he had a stroke?" His voice was tense, filled with concern as Pham came running from their bedroom with his med kit.

All the time this was going on, I was projecting my thoughts to Joshua, *I'm back, Josh. Tell them you're okay and you just had a sharp headache. You have to start talking to them or they're going to call in the EMTs.*

Caleb, is that really you? I thought something really bad happened to you. Are you okay?

I'm fine but tell them something. Don't let them think you have some serious injury.

Joshua sat up straight and said, "Wow! That was strange. I got this flash headache and lost my balance. I'm okay, really, I'm fine. Pham, just give me a couple of aspirins. Let me lie down for a few minutes but I'm fine."

Pham gave him the aspirin which he took with a glass of water, stood up from the chair without stumbling and turned and walked into his bedroom, ignoring the skeptical looks of the three of them. Sarge looked at Mark, who nodded his approval and followed Josh into the bedroom. They both laid down on the bed with Sarge resting his head on Joshua's thigh. He left the door open so everyone could see that he didn't have any repeat performances.

What the hell happened to you? he thought to me. *Are you all right?*

Yes, I'm fine. As to what happened, it's kind of sketchy. There was this spirit, a special spirit, who was some sort of judge. Carlos' spirit was there too. The judge told us the conflict between Carlos and me had to stop. Carlos told him to shove it, which really annoyed the judge so he deep sixed him, sentenced him to permanent non-existence forever. Then he rebonded us. Isn't that great news! Carlos won't be able to harass Simone or anyone else ever again.

You're right, that's fantastic news! replied Joshua.

What's fantastic news? I asked. I was getting confused.

About Carlos being destroyed, answered Joshua.

Has he been destroyed? Where did you hear about that?

Stop messing with me, Caleb. This is too important. What about the judge spirit? I had a vague memory about some kind of super spirit and answered Joshua.

Oh, him. Yeah, he said I won't remember much of what happened. He said my memory would fade or something like that. I paused. *What was I talking about?*

Nothing important, bro. I'm just glad to have by brother back and Carlos gone. He smiled as I wondered why he thought I had been gone.

A Change of Plans—Joshua

Later that morning, Simone received a call from one of the DEA agents. She told her the FBI discovered a mole in their organization and our plans may need to be changed. An all-hands meeting was set up for later in the afternoon at the DEA facility in downtown New Orleans.

When our team arrived, we were escorted to a large, secure conference room. By the time the meeting started, the room was filled to capacity. The FBI senior agent was the first to speak. "Good afternoon, I'm senior agent Jack Kramer, lead FBI agent for this mission. I'm sorry to have to inform you we discovered a mole in our organization who works for one of the lesser drug cartels, based in Panama. They refer to themselves as the Panama Cartel.

"We believe the mole passed on at least some of our plans to his cartel contact. We don't know exactly how much of the plan was revealed. Unfortunately, the mole was killed by one of the rival cartels over some other non-related cartel activities. We were surveilling the mole to see who he contacted, when he was killed.

"We don't know for a certainty he passed any information about our mission before he was killed, however we do know that several of the cartels have been observed receiving shipments of a substantial number of RPGs here in New Orleans. Our belief is these are intended to be use to shoot down the Air Force C-130 aircraft before they're able to spray the sleeping gas."

During the next few hours we discussed a variety of approaches to counter attack possible uses of the RPGs. We arrived at a multitiered approach which permitted us the greatest flexibility.

Simone took the floor to show the locations the DEA and FBI agents would use to wait undetected in the vegetation close to the river. She was very focused on her presentation with no signs of PTSD. Having Carlos out of her life was going to be a blessing. She completed that portion of her briefing by informing everyone the Coast Guard volunteered to deliver the agents by boat to their designated locations.

She finished her briefing by relating the local police SWAT teams would be a backup for taking out potential shooters while the feds were cuffing the unconscious cartel soldiers. A large number of buses used to transport prisoners would pick up and deliver all those cartel solders to various prison facilities in and around New Orleans.

After the meeting was adjourned, we headed back to our hotel to discuss the issue further. I kept wondering if there were other moles out there, possibly working for the top cartels who now know all our plans. I hoped not but I sent Caleb out on a recon mission to find out.

While Caleb was gone, the rest of us began looking at our surveillance data being recorded by the bugs we planted in the Harrah's penthouses and conference rooms. In addition, we had managed to plant additional bugs in the rooms in the Marriott used by the real El Mayo and his high-level bosses. To speed up the process, Pham was using a software app which flagged certain key words for us to review. The vast majority of the information didn't reveal anything we didn't already know except for a couple of items. First, they were going to use a non-lethal gas instead of poison. Secondly, they were going to use a CH-47

Chinook heavy-lift helicopter to haul all the unconscious bosses from the top of Harrah's in one trip to Gatorland-USA. The twin-rotor copter could carry up to fifty people at a time, just enough to fit all fifty of the cartel leaders and major bosses from the five largest cartels in the Western Hemisphere.

Rehearsal for Monday Night's Party—Mark

After we had finished our review of the bug data, Joshua had Pham and I headed over to Harrah's to get a look at the rehearsal of the big blow-out party El Mayo was putting on. It was by invitation only and included everyone from all of the cartels including soldiers and support staff. The invitation list had over two hundred names, most of which were aliases.

Pham had forged IDs showing we were with the city inspector's office there to check if all the equipment they had brought in met the city code requirements. It gave us the opportunity to check out all of their equipment. And what a collection they had. Neither Pham nor myself could determine what half of the stuff was for. So we waited patiently as we pretended to be checking out the equipment we did recognize. When everything was assembled and ready for a dry run, they turned down the house lights and fired it up. Boy, were we impressed.

The first act was a spectacular laser-light show that was synced to ear-splitting rock music. We were told it wouldn't seem so loud when there were a couple of hundred bodies acting as sound suppressors. However, as we stood there not protected by anything, I could feel my internal organs undergoing sympathetic vibrations. It felt like I was coming apart from the inside out. I looked over at Pham and discovered he had put on sound suppressing earmuffs. He handed me a pair and when I put them on, it cut down the sound level to a tolerable level.

After about ten minutes of light show, the real entertainment began. John, Paul, George and Ringo appeared on stage and began performing all of their music, from ballads to butt kicking rock and roll. Not only entertaining, it looked and sounded like they were real instead of 3-D holographic projections. We were standing less than ten feet from the stage and neither of us could tell they weren't real people. Between songs they chatted with each other as if they were performing at a live concert.

When *I Want to Hold Your Hand* finished, one of the sound crew came up to me and asked me to talk with John for a few minutes so they could check some things out. I thought he was kidding. The technician turned to John and said, "Hey John, one of your fans is here, his name is Mark."

John turned and looked me in the eyes and said, "Hello Mark, do you have a favorite song of ours you'd like us to play for you?"

The voice sounded just like John. I got tongue tied but Pham stepped in and said, "Could you play *A Hard Day's Night?'*

John turned to look at Pham and asked, "And who may you be?"

"My name is Pham," he answered.

"Isn't Pham a Vietnamese name?" he asked Pham.

"Yes sir it is, Mr. Lennon."

"Call me John, Mr. Lennon was my dear old dad."

John turned to Ringo and said, "Let's play the song for our Vietnamese friend."

Ringo started the drumbeat as the group began the song. I felt like a kid again at a concert talking to the real John Lennon. As they sang, George motioned to one of the stage hands and they handed me and Pham microphones and told us to sing along. And we did … to every song they sang in their first set. It was the most fun I ever had with my clothes on.

When the Fab Four finished their first set the tech paused the performance to check on some additional technical details and Pham approached him with a ton of questions, the first one being, "How do you get them to interact with the audience?"

The tech replied to Pham as he continued adjusting various settings, "Obviously, they're not only prerecorded holographic projections, they're avatars. There are actors in one of the adjacent conference rooms who are performing live all the movements you just watched. We overlay the image of each musician and use lip sinking when they are performing their songs. We have several stagehands who control each image when they aren't performing. That's how we get them to look at you and carry on a conversation. Each stagehand is equipped with a voice duplicator. When you hear John speak to you, the voice duplicator modifies the stagehand's voice to sound exactly like John."

Once the tech had completed her adjustments, they turned the Beatles back on. Before they appeared to be leaving the stage, Paul introduced the next act, "Let's hear it for The Rolling Stones!"

And so it went for the next hour. After the Beatles and the Stones were done preforming, the other groups sang only a few songs before they moved on. We lost count how many famous groups performed. The last group drew our undivided attention. The tech said to us, "Our last act is Carlos. You're going to love this!"

I looked over at Pham as a cold chill ran down my back. He looked as shocked as I felt. But after Carlos began, we were laughing our asses off. It was really Carlos, at least it was his avatar. However, it wasn't our Carlos. It was Carlos Santana and he was fantastic.

It turns out the techs used code words to identify the various groups, the Beatles were called Bugs, the Rolling Stones were Rocks and Carlos Santana was just Carlos. When we figured this out, we just relaxed and enjoyed the show. Carlos Santana was one fine guitarist.

When the music groups were finished, we drifted over to a second stage where the X-rated scenes were playing. We only watched the scene with Rosario Dawson from the movie *Trance.* Again, it was like we were in her bedroom watching her having sex with the leading man. You could walk around the stage and view the action from every angle. After a few minutes we decided we'd had enough for the evening and headed back to the Marriott after signing off all their equipment was up to code.

When we got back to our suite, we briefed Joshua and Simone on what we'd seen. If I remember right, we 'forgot' to mention the sex scenes.

This was going to be the party of a life time. They must have spent a fortune to produce such great special effects. I'm sure they didn't get permission to make all the avatar rock stars or replay the sex scenes but I guess they didn't have to worry about it. The creators of this show were going to become millionaires selling their creations on the dark web.

End of the Day—Joshua

It had been a very long, eventful day. The next couple of days were going to be even longer and more eventful. Everything seemed to be coming together but there was always the possibility things could go sideways in a heartbeat. I think we have a good plan with built in contingencies to cover the surprises, however we have to be flexible enough to deal with the unforeseen.

As it got later into the evening I began thinking about all the good things that had happened today. The two things that immediately came to mind, were the return of Caleb and end of Simone's PTSD.

I had been really troubled about maybe losing Caleb. I wouldn't know how to survive without him. It's been such a blessing to have him with me.

Simone's behavior vastly improved after our get together with Pastor Tom. It's been the difference between night and day for her. I also believe the removal of Carlos' spirit played a major role in that recovery.

I really wish Caleb was permitted to remember what went on with the Judge and Carlos. It's just a preference, having him back with me is all that really matters.

<u>Spying on the Sinaloa Cartel—Caleb</u>

What a relief to be back in action. To be honest, I wasn't sure I was going to continue to exist. What a joy to get rid of Carlos for ever and ever, amen. I just wish I could remember what happened to him. In retrospect, perhaps it's better to not know all the details.

I spent a large part of Sunday evening with El Mayo and his five major bosses, in the Marriott's small conference room with the 80-inch TV. I decided to give each of the bosses' nicknames. El Mayo is Jefe, the other five are now Larry, Moe, Curly, Huey, and Dewey. When I checked out their rap sheets, they had killed or had been responsible for the death of close to two hundred people. These aren't people I'd want to party with.

Speaking of parties, I was in the small conference room watching the rehearsal of the various entertainment that is to take place tomorrow night. It was pretty spectacular. I saw Mark and Pham hanging out with the Beatles. They were both wearing earmuffs to muffle the sound when the bands were preforming. What a couple of wusses. To really appreciate Rock and Roll, it needs to be loud, screaming loud.

I watched the rehearsal through the eyes of each of the bosses. I started with Dewey, but all he was interested in was a naked Rosario Dawson. I could understand the appeal but how can you ignore the Beatles? Shameless!

I read the minds of each man, taking note of any information regarding their plan but that didn't come until the rehearsal was over. Then Jefe took over.

While the others got up to refresh their drinks, Jefe summarized what he wanted to happen at the party. "I want every door to the ballroom locked down except the doors in the front. There are four doors facing the hallway and I want two of our men on each door. They will have checklists on their iPads and nobody will be allowed in unless their name is on the list. Once they match the person with the name, they will do a thorough search for any weapons and I mean any type of weapons. Guns, knives, tasers, stun guns, brass knuckles and clubs aren't permitted. If they find any weapons they will be confiscated."

One of the bosses, I think it was Dewey, asked, "What about drugs?"

"No drugs allowed," replied Jefe.

Moe asked, "What do we do with them if they have weapons or drugs?"

Jefe answered, "Once we're sure they are clean, we smile and let them inside, maybe say enjoy your evening. I want as many soldiers from every cartel at that party. I want them to enjoy themselves, have a good time, get good and drunk, let them drink until they pass out in their own puke. So, the next day they are really hung over and not a hundred percent when we drop the hammer on them."

"What should we do if they start fighting?" asked Curly.

"Stop them," replied Jefe. "Pair them up with the closest bitch to get their mind off fighting."

"Are any of the cartel bosses going to be on the list?" asked Larry.

"Yes, all the bosses' names are on the list but I seriously doubt any of the bosses from the top five cartels will show up," answered Jefe. "They are going to be focused on our meeting the next day.

"Once everyone's inside, we shut the doors and lock them down. Nobody goes in or out until the party's over. Once they lock the doors I expect you all to join me here to watch the party. Any other questions?"

There were none.

Jefe walked them to the door and said as they left, "Let's meet tomorrow morning for breakfast. If you think of any other questions we can discuss them then. You all have a good night."

I was inside Jefe's mind as he walked the short distance to his own suite. He had been wearing another Mission Impossible mask. It looked pretty good. I was going to have to suggest to Joshua we get one of the mask maker machines. I think it would come in handy.

I stayed with Jefe while he walked inside his suite and headed for the bedroom and his pretend wife. She was lying on their bed in a very sheer negligee with a glass of champagne in her hand. She handed it to El Mayo and began to undress him as he drained the bubbly. Then they fell into bed and began rutting like animals. I watched for a few moments but decided she was no Rosario Dawson. However, she was good enough for El Mayo. Since his mind was no longer focused on the cartel I decided to go back to our room.

All and all, it had been a very interesting day.

DAY 13

<u>Now I Lay Me Down to Sleep—Caleb</u>

Spirits don't sleep. When the human we are bonded to goes night-night, we have a variety of options. First on my list is to meditate. I find it has a calming effect on me. It allows me the opportunity to sort out the important things in my existence. The second thing is to pray. My papa was a Southern Baptist minister and he taught me and Joshua how to pray when we were just wee tikes. When we were at that age where we could understand certain words but were really limited in our own vocabularies, papa would put us to bed every night. Joshua and I shared the same bed then and papa would tuck us in and say this prayer:

> Now I lay me down to sleep
> Pray the Lord my soul to keep
> If I should die before I wake
> I pray the Lord my soul to take.

As we grew older and learned to speak, we would say the prayer with our papa. A little time after that, when we were old enough to understand what we were praying, we were afraid to go to sleep. We didn't want to die and have the Lord take our souls. We'd fight to stay awake and felt like zombies most of the next day. After a few sleepless nights we told papa why we were trying not to sleep.

He explained to us we weren't going to die, at least not for a good while. It was just to be sure if something did happen to us in the night, we would still be saved. By the time we started kindergarten, we finally believed him.

The next prayer he had us memorize was called the Lord's Prayer. It was the prayer Jesus used to teach his disciples how to pray. It was short and sweet and later on, when we were old enough to say our own prayers, papa said to keep our prayers short. "Just think of it like having a conversation with God." He said it might be a one-sided conversation but one way or another, God always answers our prayers.

As we prepared for going in harm's way, I put my prayers before meditation. I asked God to protect us and for us to do the right thing and "if we die and do not wake, we pray the Lord our souls to take."

Very early on Monday morning, I had finished my prayers and began to meditate. I cleared my mind and let my subconscious thoughts and feelings bubble up to the surface. Before the sun rose over New Orleans, I began to get a tickle of a feeling. It was very weak but I sensed it was slowly growing in intensity. As the first rays of sunlight peaked over the horizon, I realized it was another disturbance in the force.

This one had a different taste to it, metaphorically speaking of course. It wasn't like the spirit of Carlos, filled with anger and hatred. This one was totally devoid of emotions but as it grew closer, I could feel it was very old and very strong. Instinctively, I knew this disturbance was being created by a very old spirit, a senior spirit.

As it approached me, it felt like a tsunami, a giant wave, building in intensity. As it crashed over me, I swear I heard a deep bass gong followed by the sound of a door slamming shut.

There was the sound of ringing in my metaphorical ears which diminished with time. When the ringing stopped I realized what had happened; I had been surrounded by a shield. Apparently, it was a selective shield; a quick test revealed I could still interact with Joshua and read the minds of Simone, Mark and Pham and even Sarge (that dog has some interesting thought patterns). However, I was completely shielded from the thoughts of any of the cartels. That was going to make the next two days more difficult for the good guys.

I waited for Joshua to wake before informing him of what had happened to me. His reaction was not unexpected. *Holy crap!!! Can you shut off the shield?"*

I've been working on it but so far everything I've attempted hasn't had any effect."

True to form, Joshua ordered, *Try harder. We really need your intel.*

While Joshua and the rest of our crew got up and completed their morning routine, I made a visit to El Mayo, aka Jefe. I could still see him but only in somewhat of a blurry image. I couldn't hear him at all. It was just as well; he was getting all hot and bothered with is pretend wife again. I left the two love birds, more like vultures than love birds, and headed to Chuy and Chapo's room with the same results. I tried to connect to them to read their thoughts but got nothing. Either they had no thoughts or I was completely shielded from their minds. I figured the latter was probably the case but I was tempted to think these two body guards had no thoughts at all.

As I moved back to our suite, I realized there might be some way to bypass the shield. Being able to see even a blurry image of them was encouraging. I went to work looking for a solution.

Final Check: Battlefield & Equipment—Joshua

We split up and each one of us covered a different aspect of the mission. Simone met with the DEA agents to do a dry run on how to take down El Mayo and his bosses at the Marriott. That also included neutralizing their body guards. They practiced several approaches based on various scenarios. After a few hours they felt comfortable they had all their bases covered.

Next, she worked with the FBI and DEA agents who would make the arrests of the cartel soldiers at the battlefield site. She reminded everyone to check out their gas masks for proper fit before going after the soldiers. She brought in the Coast Guard to brief them on how they would be picking up the agents and dropping them off at their specific locations.

Lastly, she met with the drivers of the criminal transport buses to go over the protocol for handling the soldiers. She assumed most of them would be semiconscious from being gassed. She reminded them all of these man and women were known killers and to never assume they won't resist.

I sent Pham to check out the War Wagon. I wanted to be sure she (the War Wagon, of course) had her diesel tank topped off and her propulsion batteries fully charged. I wanted him to check out every weapon system on board and to verify all ammunition stores fully loaded. That included the attack drones and our own sleeping gas canisters. I also wanted him to be sure we had our own gas masks on board and functional.

When Pham arrived at our secure storage site, he was in for a surprise. He called me and gave me the sitrep. "Boss, it appears we had visitors in the early morning who attempted to break into the War Wagon."

"Were they successful?" I asked.

"No sir, they weren't. In fact they are still unconscious. There are military medics treating them as I speak," he replied.

"How many were there?"

"Three boss. Two were taken out by the wagon's security system when they attempted entry. The 250,000-volt stun security system worked as advertised. The third guy panicked in his attempt to escape when the alarm sounded and his buddies were twitching next to the wagon. It appears he tripped over one of the bodies and did a header into a nearby support column. He's also unconscious and suffering from a severe concussion. How do you want me to handle them?"

"Wait one," I replied as I called for Caleb. *Bro, I want you to transport to where Pham is and see if you can see clearly enough to identify the perps.*

Roger that, he replied and was gone. A second later he was in my head. *On site now. I think I recognize them as cartel soldiers but not sure. Let me try something. Have Pham take a really close look at them and take pictures of their faces.*

I asked Pham to see if he could identify the three men. He looked closely and took pictures of them but said he couldn't identify any of them. He would need to compare their pictures with the mug shots in the mission statement.

Caleb had a faster way. *That works for me. They're all from the Panama Cartel. Apparently, the shield only works when I look directly at them. I got a clear picture of them from reading Pham's mind and also looking at the pictures he took.*

Once the medics had finished with them, the MPs arrested them and took them to the brig. They would be out of action for several days.

Pham, after carefully deactivating the security system, began his inspection of the War Wagon while Caleb transported back to me. I had a question for him. *Why would soldiers from the Panama Cartel be involved with this. Aren't they minor players in this dance? They're not even invited to the conference, are they?*

Sorry, Josh. I wish I could help you with this but I need a little more time to come up with a fix. In the meantime, why don't you go old school on them. Maybe a physical interrogation of the men who tried to violate your War Wagon could be persuaded to part with the information you desire.

You mean torture? I asked.

Whatever works. We don't have enough time to play patty-cake with these dudes. You might get fast results with a few broken fingers, Caleb replied.

You volunteering for finger breaking?

I thought I heard the sound of a sad sigh, then Caleb thought to me, *Bro, I would if I could but I can't so I won't. So sorry.*

I'll take your suggestion under advisement. Right now, Mark, Sarge and I are going to take a trip to the crop duster strip. Want to come along? We might take another ride in the Stearman…Caleb are you still there? There was no reply.

We took the rental car out to the dirt runway the crop dusters used. I wasn't sure if Norm was there but wanted to pick his brain if he was. Mark took Sarge and headed out in the direction of Gatorland—USA while I walked into the hangar.

"Hey Norm, you here?"

"Of course," came his reply. "Where the hell else would I be?"

I told him as much as I could about what was going to happen tomorrow and strongly suggested he find some place to be out of harm's way. His response was, "No way I'm going to miss out on that action. I have a score to settle with a couple of those bastards."

I took a closer look and noticed he had a shiner over his left eye. "You okay?" I asked.

"Fine, just pissed off at those arrogant Mexicans. They wanted me to fly them around the land between here and Gartorland. I politely refused. I told them I was just a mechanic, not a pilot and they'd have to wait until after Mardi Gras for the ride when the pilots came back. They didn't like that answer so one of their big guys punched me in the eye. I told him he hit like a girl and kicked him in the nuts."

"What happened next?"

"One of the damned Mexicans took out a machine gun and shot up the Stearman. They said it was a present. They said now I could go to work and fix the plane. Damned Mexicans."

"I think you were very lucky they didn't kill you," I said. "By the way, I think they're from Panama, not Mexico."

He spat on the ground and looked at me with a hard expression. "In my book, anyone who speaks Spanish is a Mexican."

We talked for a while longer. I asked him if Gatorland was open on Mardi Gras. He said, "Nope, pretty much everything is shut down on that day. I'm shutting down too but I've got a hidey-hole up on the hanger mezzanine. I'm just going to lock myself in with a few of my own weapons to keep me company. If I see anything important, I'll call you. I've still got your business card. I'll miss the big parade but that's okay. I don't need to see the women tourists flashing their naked boobs just to get a plastic necklace or two. Good Lord, what is this world coming to?"

When Mark and Sarge had completed their rounds, we packed up the and headed back into the city.

Final Preparation—El Mayo

This would be our last meeting before the big day. I was certain everything was going as planned. We met in the Marriott's small conference room at 10:00 am. We knew this would be a working brunch and coffee, milk, juices, water and soft drinks were available, Food wise, we had breakfast sandwiches, pastries and traditional breakfasts of ham, bacon and sausages served with hash browns, eggs and toast. All of this was served by a very attractive young woman who called herself Trish.

Unfortunately, she forgot the main ingredient. "Where are the frijoles?" I asked in an annoyed tone of voice. "We are from Mexico and a Mexican breakfast always has frijoles."

"I'm so sorry, sir. I'll take care of that right away. Just give me a few minutes." She took her cell phone and tapped in a number. "Hello, let me speak to Santiago." There was a brief pause then she said, "Santiago? This is Trish. We have a group of about ten guests from Mexico and they are missing frijoles for their breakfast. Can you make that your first priority? I will be coming down to pick it up. Thank you."

With that she smiled at me, turned and headed out the door to get the frijoles. I thought to myself, now, that is the way to get things done. I like this senorita, maybe I could convince her to be my second pretend wife. Unfortunately, I believe my current pretend wife would slit the throat of anyone who tried to join us in our bed. Oh well, sometimes we must make sacrifices.

Trish was back in just a few minutes with a large serving bowl of steaming frijoles. The aroma was *fantastico* and we all hurriedly piled on the beans and took our seats at the table. Trish stayed to make sure the rest of the food was to our liking. When she turned to go, I called her over and gave her a hundred-dollar bill. She began to protest but I insisted. "You have made this meal very special for us. It's the least we can do."

She thanked me and all of my bosses as well then turned and left the room. I noticed the gentle sway of her hips as she walked and thought, perhaps I should slit the throat of my present pretend wife. I'm starting to tire of her. It wouldn't be a big loss. Oh well, business first.

After we finished our delicious meal, we got down to business. We went through our planned activities step by step answering everyone's questions as we went. I emphasized that timing was crucial; we couldn't afford to be either early or late. Everything must be done on time. My only worry was it was a very complicated plan but if, no, not if, when we succeeded we would be rich beyond our wildest dreams. Not only the richest but the most powerful cartel that had ever existed. El Guapo would seem like a pauper compared to our wealth. All of my major bosses shared my dream and they were willing to do anything to make sure this dream came true.

Who Is in the Panama Cartel? —Joshua

We needed to get details on this new player. I asked Caleb if he was still able to mentally make data base searches. Five minutes later, the laser printer in our suite began spitting out everything we wanted to know about them. What we found out was very confusing. These guys were nobodies. In the cartel hierarchy they were at rock bottom. True, they were expanding, merging with other small drug producers and dealers but based on a comparison with the five or six major cartels, Panama Cartel had assets barely over a million dollars. The major cartels had assets in the range of billions of dollars.

Pham was our businessman. He was an attorney and knew the law, he also knew how to decipher financial statements, none of the rest of us had a clue. Surprisingly, at least surprising to me, almost all cartels have financial specialists in their employ. Their main job is to increase and protect the assets of the cartel. Caleb was able to determine the Panama Cartel's was known as Banker Bob. How cute.

Pham knew we didn't have much time to dive into how Banker Bob handled Panama's wealth, such as it was. However, he did come across some startling information. About the time El Mayo announced this big party to divide up the Colombian cartel's wealth, the Panama Cartel received a large influx of cash from several sources over a period of a few days. Their assets went from a little over a million dollars to almost fifty million.

Who were the party or parties who made that contribution to the Panama cartel bank? We had no idea.

Pham didn't have time to track down the sources but Caleb was able to determine the cartel had added several new members to their team shortly after the new money was in Banker Bob's hand. Checking into the background of the new hires, he found out they were ex-military mercenaries. Several had received dishonorable discharges from their respective services for 'abusive behavior.' Most importantly, all were Hispanic men who had served in the US Army or Marine Corps. My first thought was these men were hired to fight a war. I wondered who would be their target, us or one of the rival cartels, maybe both.

At this point, all we could do was keep our eyes opened and be prepared for the unexpected.

Party Time! —El Mayo

Everything was ready, not only for tonight but also for the next day. This will be a Mardi Gras to be remembered for a long, long time. All of my bosses and their body guards would soon be gathering in the small conference room to watch the beginning of the party. We would have refreshments while we watched but I expected all of my bosses to remain sober. I also expected them to be in bed no later than midnight. I wanted everyone to be well rested and alert for our conference. That meeting would start promptly at noon. For our plan to be successful we needed to be on time at each segment of activity.

Promptly at 10:00 pm, the doors to Harrah's Grand Ballroom were thrown open and our guests began to file in. Each one had been thoroughly searched for weapons and drugs before entering and I was pleased with the reports that everything was proceeding in an orderly manner. I knew that wouldn't last for long.

Before everyone had entered, the music, complete with the laser light show, was fired up. The cocktail waitresses were busy handing out drinks as people filed in. It took thirty minutes for the invited guests to enter before the doors were shut and locked from the outside. My man in charge of making sure our guests were clean of weapons and drugs reported in as soon as the doors were shut. "Boss, it went just like clockwork. Nobody was packing or carrying any drugs."

"What was the head count?"

"Three hundred seventeen," he answered.

"Any bosses?"

"None. Just like you predicted."

"I want you and your men to remain on duty until the doors open. When they do, clear the ballroom of everyone as quickly as you can, that includes the staff as well as the guests. Once everyone is out, make sure the IT guys get all of our equipment out of the ballroom and relocated."

"Roger that, El Mayo."

There was no panic, everyone had been told that once they entered, they couldn't leave until all the performances ended at 3:00 am. The booze was flowing and everyone seemed to be digging the light show. When that ended at exactly 11:00 pm the house lights dimmed. A deep voice said, first in Spanish and then in English, "Good evening ladies and gentlemen. It's time for our entertainment to begin. Let me introduce to you … THE BEATLES!

The spotlights came to life, illuminating the iconic group as they began their first song *She Loves You.*

At first the crowd stood there dumbfounded. They couldn't believe what they were seeing and hearing. No one had revealed who the artists were going to be. It was supposed to be a surprise. Judging by their reaction, it was a tremendous surprise. It only took the guests a few seconds before they began screaming and singing along with the Fab Five.

And so it went for the next four hours. My bosses and I watched and listened to the first few songs. We sang along with the guests and I could tell this was going to be a major achievement in a new form of entertainment. When the first song was over, John and Paul chatted with a few of the guests close to the stage, then began their second song *I Want to Hold Your Hand.*

I turned to one of the smaller screens to watch the people who were driving the avatars. Everything appeared to be going as planned. I turned to the next screen and confirmed my security people were in the penthouse conference room where we'd be holding our meeting. I spoke briefly with them to confirm things were quiet there. The next screen showed me a picture of the helicopter landing pad. A different group of my men were making sure no one was messing with the landing area.

Everything was going exactly as planned. I allowed myself to relax a little and had one drink as the Beatles' avatars finished up their first set and Mick Jagger and the Rolling Stones began their set with *Jumping Jack Flash.* At midnight we turned in for the night.

Midnight Call—Joshua

I was just on the verge of falling asleep when my phone rang. I fumbled in the dark and located the phone. "Hello. Who's calling please?"

"Isaiah, this in Norm. Just wanted to let you know about an hour ago a fuel truck loaded with JP-4 pulled up with the lights out and just sat there. A few minutes ago, a helicopter landed and a couple of guys from the tanker truck began refueling the chopper."

"Could you tell what type of helicopter landed?"

"Of course. What kind of idiot do you think I am? It was a block 2 version of the CH-47 Chinook. What do you want me to do, take them out? Just one shot from old Betsy and the tank truck, the chopper and the Mexicans are all toast."

"Don't do anything, Norm. We need that bird to be operational tomorrow morning. Stay in your hidey-hole and remain out of site. You got me?"

There was a pause before Norm replied. When he did, he sounded disappointed. "Roger that, Isaiah."

As I hung up the phone, I thought to myself, *another piece of the puzzle falls into place.*

Caleb thought to me, *Were you calling me? Joshua?*

I vaguely heard Caleb but I drifted off to sleep before I could answer.

<u>DAY 14</u>

<u>Asking for Mercy—Caleb, 0200 hours</u>

It was the middle of the night, hours before dawn and I was frustrated. I felt like I was going into battle with both hands tied behind my back. Of course, I say that metaphorically, I have no hands to tie behind my back. Even if I did, I have no back to tie them behind. Perhaps it's best to say I was frustrated.

As I matured as a spirit, my abilities increased. I was naïve to think that trend would continue. When I got into a conflict with Carlos, a judge spirit informed me Carlos had broken the rules of spirithood. I had no idea there were any rules for spirits. Carlos learned the hard way the penalty for his violations. He no longer exists.

Just when I thought things were going to revert back to the way they were before Carlos, another senior spirit blocks me from being able to gather information on the upcoming battle. I didn't think that was fair and I decided to see if I could contact the judge.

This is the spirit of Caleb Brown, attempting to contact senior spirit, Judge Joaquin Castelan. If you get this message, please reply as soon as possible.

Immediately, I received a reply. *I'm here, spirit of Caleb Brown, how may I assist you?*

I was surprised by how quickly he responded to my request, pleased but very surprised. I found I wasn't prepared to make a request so quickly, I tried a stalling technique to give me more time to figure out what to say to him. *Um, what should I call you? Judge or Joaq…*

Call me anything you want. You didn't think this through, did you? You only have a vague idea what you really want. I know exactly what you want; you want me to take away the shield a senior spirit has placed on you. You want to have full access to thoughts of anybody you want.

I waited for him to continue. When he didn't, I said, *You're right Judge.*

Of course, I'm right. I'm always right.

Can you help me? I responded with a hint of pleading in my 'voice.'

I can but I won't. Good day to you.

I screamed at him before he could disappear, *Wait!!! Why won't you help me? If you don't, hundreds of people will die needlessly in a war we can prevent if you help me.*

I'm the judge of the actions of spirits, not flesh and blood bodies. If humans 'might die' it's no concern of mine. Are you through now?

No, I'm just getting started. Don't you dare leave me now, I said in a threatening voice. *Either you remove the shield or show me how to do it myself. Those are your only two options.*

And just who do you think you are to threaten a judge? I've been a judge for centuries. You need to watch what you say to me or you can end up like Carlos. You've been a spirit for only a few years, you don't have any idea of the limits spirits are restricted to!

Now who's making the threats? I yelled back at him.

The judge shook his head and replied in a softer manner, *They're not threats, Caleb, it's just the way things are.*

I forced myself to calm down, at least a little, then asked Joaquin, *Would you consider removing the shield for the next twenty-four hours? If you agree, in return, I'd forfeit my existence. Would that balance the scales?*

Joaquin said nothing. His image just stared at my image for what seemed like an eternity before he answered, *Are you sure this is what you want to do?*

I stared back at him with my fake eyes and shook my fake head and replied, *No, it's not what I want to do, it's what I have to do. I can't let Joshua and the rest of us die because I wasn't willing to make the sacrifice.*

After a long look at me, he said, *I'll take it under advisement.* Then he disappeared.

Early to Bed, Early to Rise—Simone

I was the first one to wake up, at least I didn't hear anyone moving yet, even Sarge was still curled up at the foot of the bed. As quietly as I could, I slipped from the bed and headed for the bathroom. I was half way there when Joshua asked, "Are you okay?"

I turned and saw him crawling out from under the covers. "I'm fine," I answered. "I need to be at DEA headquarters early. Do you need to use the bathroom before I shower?"

"No, I'm good. Take your shower. Do you need someone to wash your back?"

I smiled at him and said, "Down, lover boy. Maybe tomorrow after all this is over, okay?"

He buried his head into his pillow and pretended to be snoring as I went in the bathroom and turned on the shower.

By the time I had finished in the bathroom, everybody was up. Sarge was no longer in the bedroom, Mark probably took him out for his morning run. Pham was sitting at the desk in front of the computer, delving deeper into the Panama cartel's financial records. Thirty minutes later, Trish came in with our breakfast. I grabbed a piece of toast and a cup of coffee then headed out while the others, including Sarge, wolfed down their food.

I took a taxi to the DEA office. I felt good, really good. The last two nights I slept like a baby, not a single nightmare of any kind. In retrospect, I think Joshua's idea of speaking to Pastor Tom really made the difference. I can't believe I was so messed up I was thinking about making my nightmares come true.

If Joshua hadn't taken the Glock out of my hands, I think I would have made the worst mistake of my life. But that's all behind me now. What a difference 48 hours can make. I couldn't wait to take down so many drug cartels in a single day.

Update from Norm—Joshua

It was a little passed 0900 hours when Norm called. His voice was soft and low. "Just checking in, Isaiah. Not much happening. The Chinook was fueled at first light and the tanker truck left as soon as they were done. The chopper crew has been double checking all the bird's systems. I noticed each crew member had a gas mask attached to their belt. Any idea why?"

Instead of answering his question, I asked, "Do you have a working gas mask?"

"Sure thing," he answered.

"Keep it close to you for the rest of the day. You might need it." I changed gears and followed with another question of my own, "Are you planning on staying in your hidey hole all day?"

"If you want me to, I'll stay," he replied.

"Thanks Norm. I need you to do me a huge favor. As soon as the Chinook lifts off, call me. I need to know exactly when it leaves. About an hour after the chopper leaves, things are going to get really hairy. Promise me you'll stay put in your hidey hole. When you see the C-130s coming, put on your gas mask and don't take it off until I call you. You got all that Norm?"

"I sure as hell do." He paused and added, "This reminds me of being in Nam. I'm looking forward to helping you out."

Miracles Happen—Caleb, 0930 hours

It was happening, it started out so slowly I hardly noticed it. Within ten minutes the shield evaporated and I was back to full power. Of course, I tested every aspect of my abilities to make sure I was a hundred percent. I was momentarily stunned to find out I'd received a boost, I now had new and improved abilities. It seemed like I was now at one hundred and fifty percent. I guessed it was a gift from Joaquin.

I didn't take time to completely explore my upgrades, I had a lot of catching up to do. First thing on that list was to contact Joshua. *Joshua, the shields are down, I'm back to full strength and then some!*

His response was, *It's about time! You've got a lot of catching up to do, bro. Get with it.*

I countered with, *Say please.*

Okay, he replied, *Please dear brother of mine, I'd be ever so happy if you'd get back to work and quit screwing around.*

When you put it that way, how can I refuse? It was just like old times.

I'd been so pumped up about getting my normal spirit abilities back, I had momentarily forgotten the price I was going to pay. I mentally shrugged my shoulders and remembered what my papa taught us way back when we were just kids, "Live for today. Don't worry about anything else."

Preparations for the Conference—El Mayo

We all met in the large conference room on top of Harrah's. I, and all of my highest-ranking bosses, were wearing our masks and many of my own people didn't recognize us until we turned off our voice regulators. Of course our security people accompanied us on our short ride from the Marriott to Harrah's. I had invited them to join us for breakfast today, which I later found out was somewhat of a mistake. As soon as Trish brought in our breakfast, my pretend wife was all over me.

"Why is this *puta gringa* bringing your food?" she said in a loud enough voice all my men could hear. "She shouldn't be here, she might be a spy for the *federales*."

She had become worse than my real wife. I took her aside and told her to go back to my suite at the Marriott and get me my iPad that I had 'accidently' left there. At first, she refused, she suggested Chapo should go get it. I took her out in the hall and slapped her a few times across the face to get her attention. "You will do as I say with no backtalk or I will have you sent back to Culiacán immediately. You're my bodyguard, not my wife. You have no business being jealous just because I smile at a pretty, young girl."

Her eyes flashed at me when she heard the word young. So I slapped her a few more times and told her to remain in the suite and not come back.

I watched her walk to the express elevator. When the doors closed and it started down to the lobby, I composed myself before returning to the conference room.

Sometimes, I thought to myself, *it's unfortunate I am so irresistible to women.*

Down to business. My IT people did a dry run with the avatars. It went perfectly. I was very impressed with the quality of the images and the voices, especially mine, it sounded exactly like it was me speaking. The actors in the adjacent conference room performed flawlessly. They'd better be just as good when the real show begins at noon.

All of my security people were briefed again as to how to treat our guests. Each guest was required to be at the hotel lobby at 11:30 am where they would be escorted to the express elevators. They would search all guests for weapons and confiscate any and all of them with the promise they would be returned after the conference was concluded. The guests would then take the express elevator to the conference room where they would undergo another search, just to be sure they hadn't stashed any weapons inside the elevator or the outside shaft. After clearing the second search, my security people would escort the guests to their designated seats to wait for the conference to begin.

We next went through a dry run on dispersing the sleeping gas. We connected a supply of test gas, actually compressed air with an unpleasant odorizer and colorizer added, then locked the doors and simulated gassing the conference room. We used our own security guards as guinea pigs. They sat in random seats around the conference table. When we remotely opened the valves on the compressed air canisters, the test gas entered the conference room through the air ducts. We were able to track the pattern of the gas dispersal and time it took to reach the entire room. It took about ten seconds. I was very pleased.

We ran the simulation a second time with similar results. We brought in large portable fans and opened all the outside doors to clear any residue of the test gas. After we could no longer detect any foul odor, we shut down the fans and disconnected the test cannisters and carefully, very carefully installed the real sleeping gas bottles. Everyone wore gas masks until every canister was hooked up and leak tested.

Our last simulation was of loading the sleeping bodies into the Chinook helicopter that would arrive on the landing pad just after the sleeping gas had done its job. Again I was very pleased. The bosses had instructed their soldiers on how to quickly load the bodies. No one needed to be too concerned about being careful with the bodies, we were pretty sure the alligators wouldn't mind a bruise or two.

In planning this operation we had discussed at length whether to use sleeping gas or poison. Poison gas would be quicker and require less complexity but I really didn't want to leave dead bodies behind in the hotel. There was always the possibility of the gas not being contained in the conference room. As soon as the doors were opened the gas would probably kill many of the residents in the hotel. I really didn't want to be responsible for the collateral damage and the possibilities some of my own people might be killed. So we settled on sleeping gas.

As far as getting rid of fifty or so men was concerned, the alligators were an unexpected bonus. Once they were loaded on the helicopter it would take a little over half an hour to fly from Harrah's helipad to just beyond Gatorland

and another thirty minutes to throw out all the sleeping drug lords and cartel bosses into the waiting mouths of oh so many hungry alligators just waiting for a late lunch in the bayou.

We finished all our preparation in a little less than an hour. The conference room was cleaned and prepped for the meeting. Of course I wouldn't be at the conference room for the meeting. My bosses and I would be watching the fun from special surveillance cameras we installed in the conference rooms and in the helicopter as well.

Once the Chinook had gotten rid of the evidence with the assistance of hungry reptiles, we would quietly checkout of the Marriott hotel and return to our respective homes and families. I couldn't wait to hear the reports from my soldiers who had begun looting the banks of all our guests at the same moment the alligators were chowing down. I thought it was possible I would become the richest man in the world.

Boat Ride—Simone, 1045 hours

I watched as the DEA and FBI agents climbed aboard the Coast Guard boats and began their trips down river to their respective locations. Each agent had their gas masks strapped to their belts and a bag of zip ties to cuff the cartel prisoners, hopefully while still unconscious. Of course, they were all carrying their weapons and were dressed in battle armor. Assuming everything went according to schedule, they would be deployed well before any of the cartel soldiers appeared.

It was expected that the soldiers would be monitoring their bosses' locations as best they could. When they saw the large helicopter landing on the helipad on top of Harrah's and leaving a few minutes later, they would follow it as it flew toward Gatorland—USA. Based on the number of soldiers that had accompanied their bosses to New Orleans, we were anticipating over a hundred soldiers trying to rescue their bosses. We would be waiting for them.

We had received some intel some of the cartel soldiers might have access to a large number of RPG's. If true, we believed it would be the soldiers from the Panama Cartel who were the most likely to use them. To counter this potential threat, SWAT teams from New Orleans PD were being deployed.

I will be hooking up with my DEA team to arrest El Mayo and the Sinaloa cartel bosses at the Marriott hotel. Agents from the FBI will be at Harrah's to round up any of the Sinaloa people who remained after the helicopter departed for Gatorland.

<u>Last Minute Checking—Caleb, 1100 hours</u>

Joshua has assigned me to check on as many of the cartels as possible before the party started at noon. It felt good to be useful again.

My first assignment was to locate El Mayo and see if I could discover more details about the upcoming meeting. I went to his suite in the Marriott first but the only one there was his pretend wife, she wasn't happy. She was in a rage over how El Mayo had treated her. She had all these visions about how she would kill him. I disconnected when she began envisioning how she would emasculate him first and then feed him his testicles. That was one scary woman.

I moved on to the conference room at the top of Harrah's. He had just left but I was able to discover more details of how the meeting would be going down. Before I could find him, Joshua called me back.

He wanted to have me check on Norm, the man from the crop duster hanger who liked to fly ancient airplanes, a strange dude if I ever saw one.

I found him in a small room in the upper level of the hangar. He was dressed for combat with a flak vest and enough weapons to fight a small war. Besides the machine gun, shot gun and sniper rifle, he had a variety of powerful handguns. Just like Joshua, he had two Desert Eagle 50 caliber AE semiautomatics and more boxes of ammo than a truck could carry. But I was truly surprised to see he had his own RPG and a WWII bazooka with a half dozen rockets. I pitied the fool who would even think about tangling with this dude!

Since I was in the area, relatively close to the Gatorland—USA, Joshua had me check to make sure the facility was completely shut down. He wanted to ensure there were no maintenance people working on the holiday. It was a good thing I checked. There were two men working at the hatchery area, fortunately I was able to read their minds and both were wrapping up their work and would be leaving at noon. I let Joshua know and he asked me to stay until I could confirm they had left.

While I waited, I took a quick look around the place, then ventured out into the swampland. I came upon a huge gator, he had to be well over fifteen feet and a thousand pounds. A thought occurred to me. I wondered if I would be able to read the mind of this gigantic monster. What could he possibly be thinking?

Gradually, very gradually, I slipped into his mind. I was met by pain, excruciating hunger. *I must kill and eat. Very soon I must kill and eat!*

I disengaged rapidly! My next thought was how glad I was to be spirit and not the next meal for this creature and his friends. I mentally shivered at what the cartel bosses were in for.

I headed back to the hatchery and arrived a few minutes before noon, just in time to see the two men from the hatchery get into their cars and leave for home or maybe to celebrate the last day of Mardi Gras.

After checking in with Joshua, he told me Mark, Pham and he, along with Sarge, were going to pick up the War Wagon and head out to Norm's hanger. He asked me to meet him there.

Step 1—Lobby to Conference Room—El Mayo

The cartel bosses began showing up at the express elevator a little before 11:30 am. There were ten people for each cartel. Each of the bosses of a given cartel were grouped together and quickly searched by four of my security people. After the weapons they were carrying were confiscated with the promise of return, each cartel group was hustled into the elevator along with one of my men as a chaperone.

This was repeated four additional times. Once everyone had entered into the conference room, the doors were closed and locked, including the glass doors that faced the helicopter landing pad. The pad was empty, except for my men, armed with machine guns.

I was seated on a slightly elevated platform with my bosses facing the windows where we could spot the helicopter approaching.

Up, Up & Away—Norm, 1135 hours

I'd been watching the helicopter intently since the tanker crew began their refueling. That was almost four hours ago. The helicopter crew of three had been doing a very thorough preflight check of the bird as soon as the refueling was completed and the tank truck departed.

That preflight check ended about thirty minutes ago. The last item on their checklist was to install a 50-caliber machine gun in the hatch on the port side of the bird. When they were finished, they fired off a few rounds toward the swamp, just to make sure it worked properly.

I hadn't moved from my hidey hole perch since the tanker truck left. It was a perfect spot to observe what was going on without being spotted by the crew of the chopper. At 1130 hours I could see both the pilot and copilot were in their seats and strapped in. I noticed the pilot as he talked on his radio, then reached up and hit the overhead switches which started up the two gas turbine engines. Both the forward and aft rotors began to spin up, very slowly at first but faster until they reached idle speed.

I picked up my phone and called Isaiah. "Boss, this is Norm. The Chinook is about to lift off. It should be airborne any second now."

"Roger that, Norm. Good work," was his reply.

I kept talking as the chopper slowly lifted off. "It's a few feet off the ground and hovering … Holy shit!" I screamed into the phone. "The son-of-a-bitch is strafing me."

"Get to cover, Norm!" I barely heard him yell. The noise of the waist gun was very loud.

The Chinook stopped firing and continued to climb, then dipped it's nose and began accelerating toward New Orleans. As the bird moved farther away, the sound of the engines faded and I could hear Isaiah again. "Norm, are you okay?"

"Yeah, I'm fine. No real damage, he only fired a few rounds at me as a parting gift. He's on his way to you now."

"Thanks again Norm. Take care of yourself and keep a lookout for the C-130s."

Step 2--It's a Gas, Gas, Gas—El Mayo

"Gentlemen and Ladies, welcome to the first conference of the major cartels in the Western Hemisphere. Our goal here is to form a federation of cartels who work together instead of competing with each other. Today, we will be presenting suggestions on how the federation could work together to increase profits for all cartels."

I could see the helicopter approaching the landing pad. At the same time, the large screen behind us came to life with an image of a map of the Western Hemisphere showing in red the locations of each of the six major cartels, followed in blue for what we considered as minor cartels. Background music played softly as I touched the button activating the sleeping gas canisters.

Those closest to the air ducts were the first to lose consciousness. Those farther away from the ducts had a few seconds to realize our trap had been sprung.

A few made it all the way to the locked hall doors before passing out. Several tried to escape to the helipad through the locked glass doors only to briefly see the Chinook helicopter touching down before they also fell unconscious. The only ones who seemed to be unphased by the gas were me and my bosses or should I say, our avatars weren't affected by the gas. The actors in the adjacent conference room had played their parts exceptionally well. Last night they had been, The Beatles, The Rolling Stones, Carlos Santana and many other groups and today they stood in for me and my bosses. It was a shame they had to die but I couldn't afford to leave any loose ends.

The doors to the helipad were opened by my men standing outside waiting for my signal. All of them were wearing gas masks. Large fans were brought in to clear the room of the gas. At the same time my men began carrying the unconscious men and women from the conference room and throwing then into the CH-47.

As I estimated, it took almost thirty minutes to get everyone loaded and ready for Step 3.

Busting the Bosses (almost)—Simone

All of the DEA agents had quietly moved into position outside the Marriott's small conference room and at the suites used by El Mayo and his bosses. We waited until we got the message the chopper was ready to leave Harrah's. We knew the leaders of the Sinaloa cartel had used the avatars to simulate themselves and were watching from the Marriott locations.

I had all the federal arrest warrants, thanks to Pham's efforts. We were going to hit seven locations in the Marriott at the same time to minimize any escape attempts. Each location had a leader waiting for me to give them a count down. "Ready to breach?"

As I stood in front of the small conference room, I got six double clicks acknowledging they were in position at the other locations and ready. "Five, four, three, two, one, GO!"

We rushed into the rooms and quickly subdued everyone, cuffing them all and reading them their rights. I was mildly surprised it had gone so easily. I was reading El Mayo, formally known as Ismael Zamada-Garcia, his rights and he started smiling at me.

"Why are you smiling, you're going away to a federal prison for the rest of your life? Do you think that's humorous?"

"Not at all, Agent Simone," he answered after reading my badge. "Unfortunately, you've arrested the wrong people."

"Nice try but I'm not buying it," I replied.

"Unfortunately for you, Agent Simone, I'm not Ismael Zamada-Garcia."

"Oh really, then who are you?" I asked sarcastically.

"I'm his body double. All of the men you think are his bosses are body doubles as well. The real people you want left some time ago."

I felt my heart sink. "Where did they go?" I asked in as calm a voice I could manage.

"El Mayo didn't share that information with me but I assume he went back to his villa in Sinaloa. Better luck next time."

I was driving the War Wagon, on our way to the crop duster strip, when Simone called and informed me that El Mayo was in the wind along with his bosses. She informed me they had pulled a last-minute switch with their respective body doubles. She had ordered a BOLO, (Be On the Look Out), for them but she wasn't too hopeful they would turn up. The good news was a lot of his soldiers were arrested and hoped it would make a considerable dent in their operation.

After she had disconnected, I put out a call to Caleb. I relayed to him the information Simone had given me and then asked, *With your new superpowers, do you think you could locate the real El Mayo?*

Of course, bro. Any ideas as to where he and his crew had escaped too?

His body double suggested he might already be back in Sinaloa but I doubt it. I think he's laying low in New Orleans waiting for the searches to die down before he makes any moves.

I'll get right on it. I'll contact you as soon as I get something.

We were making good time heading to the crop duster strip. I wanted to check on Norm first, then watch for the soldiers we expected to show up. The one thing I was concerned about was the Panama cartel and what their game was. At this point there were many possibilities.

I had Mark searching for the Chinook using the War Wagon's radar system. About five minutes later, Mark sang out, "Talley ho! Radar contact, estimate they're fifteen minutes behind us, en route to Gatorland."

As we turned off the highway and headed to the crop duster hangar, I noticed several vehicles closing on us at a fast rate. "Check our six, Mark. I think we might have company."

Pham looked up from his computer screen and said, "Bad news, Joshua. I just found out who's sponsoring the Panama cartel. You aren't going to like the answer."

"Give it to me anyway," I said.

"It's one of our federal friends, not sure which one. It will take a lot more work to find out which agency."

Mark and I turned to briefly stare at Pham. Mark said, "You've got to be shitting me. Our own feds are funding the bad guys?"

"Yes indeed," he answered.

Mark interrupted. "That traffic following us has very new versions of an armored personnel carrier, specifically, a heavily modified Arques Fortress Armored Personnel Carrier. The additions appear to be 50-caliber machine guns mounted in turrets, grenade launchers and rocket tubes. And they just turned off the highway and are coming this way. It appears they have some type of logo on the doors but I can't make them out."

We had parked in the back of the hangar and weren't sure if they were coming after us or had some other target in mind. They passed the hangar making good speed, traveled to the end of the dirt strip and turned toward Gatorland. About a mile south of the runway they split up heading east and west and ended up facing north, spaced about a half mile apart.

It wasn't long before we could hear the thump-thump of the Chinooks twin rotors as it headed toward the swamp's gator infested dumping grounds. Pham had moved to the weapons control seat and informed me, "They're going to shoot down the chopper if we don't stop them."

I drove the War Wagon out from behind the hangar and headed toward the center APC. I could see the 50-caliber machine guns tracking the helicopter. He was almost in range when I order Pham, "Take them out, now!"

"Roger that, boss." A few seconds later, we heard the sounds of three guided rockets fired from their launch tubes. Several seconds after that, the rockets hit their targets, destroying the APCs.

We drove out to the debris field to see if there were any survivors. We found fifteen dead and three survivors. There was no time for briefing as the CH-47 flew over our heads and continued toward Gatorland.

Tag, You're It—Caleb, 1255 hours

I was trying out my new abilities when I found El Mayo and his senior bosses. All I had to do was to focus, really focus on him, and after a few seconds, it could have been milliseconds, time is really messed up for us spirits, whatever time it took, his location stood out like a blinking red light on a locator map.

They were in Gatorland waiting to be picked up by a fast cigarette boat which was just starting to navigate from the Gulf into the bayou. They were all gathered in the Gatorland dining hall as they waited. I discovered they had some strange items on the menus scattered about on the tables. Who in their right mind would want to eat a Gator Burger?

I forwarded my find to Joshua, who in turn contacted Simone who had moved on from the Marriott to oversee the agents waiting for the soldiers. She and a half dozen agents separated from their group, commandeered a vehicle and headed to the Gatorland dining hall.

Step 3.5—A Diversion—El Mayo

We heard the sounds of rockets exploding and I immediately contacted the pilot of the Chinook to find out what was going on. He told me he was under imminent attack. Several vehicles had been shooting at him before they were destroyed by some unknown vehicle. He indicated he was going to change course and approach the swamp from a different direction to avoid further attacks.

I approved his plan but indicated he must dump his cargo in the swamp before I leave Gatorland by boat, no more than twenty minutes from now.

Lots & Lots of Soldiers—Joshua, 1300 hours

They were coming in by the truck loads, soldiers looking to save their leaders. When the helicopter had diverted away from the main highway, they went four-wheeling across the grassland to keep the chopper in sight. I kept searching the sky for my surprise. Finally, I saw them, two A-10 Warthogs from England AFB in Alexandria, Louisiana. They were part of a National Guard unit based there. They descended on the Chinook helicopter like two hawks after a pigeon, forcing the bird to land before it reached Gatorland.

The A-10s were designed for close air support missions; they flew low and slow to defend our troops on the ground. One version was referred to as The Tank Killer. They were equipped with a nose mounted Gatling gun firing depleted uranium bullets that penetrated tank armor giving the tanks the appearance of swiss cheese. These two Warthogs had the standard 30 mm Gatling gun used to strafe enemy soldiers.

On their first pass of the helicopter they tried contacting the chopper's pilot but he didn't respond until the lead plane pitched away from the chopper then circled back and fired a burst of bullets across it's bow. That certainly got the pilot's attention and he landed immediately.

The cartel soldiers swarmed the grounded bird as the two A-10s left the scene and returned to base. The soldiers quickly killed the flight crew and began dragging their unconscious leaders out of the bird and laid them on the ground, waiting for them to recover.

We noticed some skirmishes breaking out between the soldiers from different cartels. This was going to escalate into a full fledge war if we didn't do something.

"Time for the C-130s," I said to no one in particular.

"Here they come," said Norm a few minutes later as we all put on our gas masks.

We could hear the deep rumbling sounds from the C-130s' turboprop engines and they kept getting louder as the four aircraft approached what we called the killing field. They flew directly over the hangar at about five hundred feet above us. They were so close everything in the hangar was vibrating and rattling as the sound reached its peak.

As they passed over the hangar, we watched as the four planes dropped down even lower, extended full flaps and deployed their landing gear, slowing the planes to a near-stall velocity. They spread out into an echelon right formation that covered the entire battlefield. At about a hundred yards from the large group of cartel soldiers they began dusting the area with the sleeping gas.

The soldiers stopped fighting with each other and stood almost transfixed for a few seconds at the sight of the four aircraft bearing down on them. When the spraying began, most of them panicked and ran for their vehicles in an attempt to escape.

One cartel pickup truck with several soldiers in the bed turned towards the lead plane. One of the men hoisted an RPG onto his shoulder. As he fired, the truck hit a large ditch which ran across the field, crashing the front of the truck into the opposite embankment. The man with the RPG was thrown out of the truck bed and the RPG exploded harmlessly into the ground.

After the first pass by the C-130s, the sleeping gas had sent most of the cartel soldiers into la-la land. Just before the aircraft reached Gatorland, they turned off the spray, raised flaps and gear, pulled up into a 180 degree turn and made a second pass going north. When they completed the second pass, all of the soldiers were lying unconscious on the battlefield.

The C-130s wagged their wings as a salute and returned to base.

El Mayo and the Gators—Caleb, 1345 hours

With my new superpowers, I was able to monitor both El Mayo and his bosses as well as Simone and her agents simultaneously. El Mayo was in a rage as he watched all of his planning flushed down the toilet. He had lost everything. His only hope now was to escape back to Sinaloa.

The cigarette boat had almost reached the bayou dock. As they stood waiting on the dock, a minivan pulled up in front of the Gatorland entrance. It was the DEA, being led by a woman he recognized as Simone. Apparently, she was much more than the reservation clerk who worked at Harrah's hotel.

His anger intensified, now his hope for reaching asylum in Sinaloa was hopeless. Not only would he and his men not reach their homeland, they would be arrested by a woman. That was the last straw.

"Kill them," he shouted to his men. "Kill them all!" he ordered, knowing there was no chance of survival. The gunfire was deafening. There was no place to hide, no place to shield themselves, one by one they fell, mortally wounded.

I melded with El Mayo, his mind a cacophony of anger and fear. I planted a thought, "Escape! Run away. You can make it. The boat is close. You can jump on it and escape. Hurry, run now!!!

At the same time, I planted a thought in the primitive mind of the monster gator. He had followed the boat as it wound its way through bayou towards the dock. *Follow the boat. Food is coming. You're so hungry!*

El Mayo turned and ran down the dock toward the boat. The boat pilot had put the boat in reverse to distance himself from the gun battle. He was at least ten feet from the dock when El Mayo launched himself into the air at the very end of the dock. In that instant of time he realized the pilot had started to move off in the boat; he would end up in the swamp! Just before he hit the water, he shot and killed the pilot for leaving him.

When he hit the water his gun flew from his hand. He had to make it to the boat and began swimming furiously, pounding the water. He was closing the distance when he struck a submerged log or something that blocked his path to the boat. He tried to climb over it but the 'log' rose up and engulfed his head in its giant mouth, pulling him under the water.

The monster gator began rolling, twisting El Mayo's head free from his body. It crushed the head in its powerful mouth and swallowed the fragments. He was just getting started and within a few minutes, it had consumed the entire body. Satisfied, he turned and slowly swam back into the swamp to rest. He was no longer hungry.

All that remained of El Mayo was spreading pool of his blood on the surface of the water.

Picking Up the Pieces—Simone, 1415 hours

Once the C-130s were finished with their spraying, the DEA and FBI agents moved in and began securing the unconscious cartel soldiers. We didn't attempt to determine which cartel they belonged to, we just wanted to make sure they were cuffed before they regained consciousness and any weapons they might be carrying were confiscated.

It took over an hour for most of the prisoners to regain consciousness. As soon as they were able to stand up and walk (or stumble) they were escorted to the prison buses and transported to a central facility for processing. We estimated we arrested two hundred fifty men and women, including the drug lords and cartel bosses. We had federal arrest warrants for many of them which included their names and photographs which made it relatively easy to match the prisoner with the warrant. The others took more time to identify.

It took several hours to remove all the prisoner from the battlefield. Only one of the bosses from the Sinaloa cartel survived the gun battle at Gatorland—USA. He was severely wounded and not expected to survive. No remains of El Mayo were recovered. The number of deaths recorded was surprisingly small. In addition to the three CH-47 crew, the five Sinaloa bosses and two men who were killed when their pickup truck ran into a ditch, only six additional deaths were recorded, none were collateral damage.

My relief arrived an hour into the arrest process and I was able to join up with Joshua's team back at the duster strip hangar.

Winding Down—Joshua, 1630 hours

It was late afternoon and the sun had begun drifting behind a bank of clouds causing shadows to fall over the hangar. Norm had climbed down from his hidey hole still wearing his body armor and gas mask, carrying his sniper rifle slung over his shoulder and an Uzi machine pistol in his right hand.

"Hey Mark," Norm called out as he pulled the mask from his face. "How 'bout you put some ice from my freezer into yonder tub and slide it over here. I think I have a few cases of beer somewhere in the back. Wearing that damned mask all day has plum dried me out."

Simone and Mark started opening up the cases of beer and putting the cans into the tub of ice. "Where's Sarge?" I asked Mark.

He pointed toward the battlefield. "He's out there chasing every critter he can find. Once he catches one he lets it go and searches for new game. This is fun time for him but it's also good training. When he gets tired he'll come join us."

We pulled up some folding chairs and sat around a fire pit off to one side of the front of the hangar. It was starting to get a bit nippy as the sun moved lower towards the bayou. Norm threw some logs into the pit and sprayed on what he called fire starter which smelled very similar to gasoline. He used a torch to start the fire. There was a *woof* sound as the logs burst into flames.

I opened a can of lukewarm beer, raised it high and proposed a toast. "To a very successful mission. It couldn't have gone any better. We accomplished everything we set out to do and then some. Thank you all for your help. It took all of us and a lot of other men and women to make this happen."

"To a successful mission," said Mark and he took a sip of his beer, Norm and Simone joined him.

"Where's Pham?" I asked no one in particular.

"He's in the War Wagon," Simone replied. "He's working on the computer. He told me he's close to finding out who's been funding the Panama cartel."

After our second round of Coors, Sarge came back to join us and laid down at Mark's feet. I noticed he was still wearing his doggie battle armor.

Norm commented, "Your dog looks plum tuckered out."

Mark reached down and petted Sarge as Simone scrounged a bowl, filled it with water and placed it on the ground in front of Sarge. He immediately began lapping it up until he had drunk it all. Simone asked him, "Still thirsty, big guy?" Sarge barked once in agreement and Simone gave him a refill.

Pham had just finished up his work on the War Wagon's computer. He didn't look happy as he walked to join us at the fire pit.

"Why so glum, Pham?" asked Mark.

He didn't get a chance to answer. The RPG struck the back of the hangar a split second after Caleb screamed into my mind, *INCOMING! Get down!*

I echoed his warning and we all dove for cover.

The first rocket was followed by a second round, then a third. The entire wooden hangar was engulfed in flames as well as several of the vintage aircraft.

I heard Mark yell to Sarge, "Sarge, search and destroy. SEARCH and DESTROY!!!" The wolf-dog took off like a streak around the right side of the building.

Norm bounced to his feet like a man half his age, took one look at the burning aircraft and began ranting. "Those sons a bitches. I'm going to kill every one of those bastards." He took off at a dead run around the left side of the hangar, holding the Uzi at the ready, safety off.

Mark, Simone and I ran toward the War Wagon which hadn't been touched by the RPGs. Pham was lying on the ground, not moving. *Caleb, how's Pham?*

Unconscious, badly beaten up … broken collar bone on his left side … internal bleeding. He may not make it, was his reply.

Simone was the closest thing to an EMT we had. She knew it and didn't wait for me to ask. She was in the War Wagon in a flash and exited just as fast with a med kit in her hand. Mark and I jumped into the War Wagon and fired her up. I drove around the left side of the burning hangar accelerating into the war zone. Mark was in the weapons operator area and had everything ready to fire.

The first thing we saw was Sarge as he attacked not one but two men holding empty RPG launchers. One was already down and not moving. As we roared by him I could see his throat had been ripped out. The second man had tried running away but Sarge had caught up with him and jumped on his back knocking him to the ground. He had his massive jaws locked on the man's neck shaking him the way a puppy shakes a stuffed toy. If the man wasn't dead, he soon would be.

Fifty yards away, Norm was in a firefight with three other men, mercenaries by the looks of their gear. They were all wearing body armor and advancing on Norm with automatic weapons fire.

The lead merc began running toward Norm screaming like a mad man, until Norm shot him in the head with his sniper rifle. Norm had been less than a hundred yards away from the man when he fired and the 50-caliber bullet which turned the merc's head into a red mist. Even without his head he continued to run a couple of more steps before he toppled to the ground.

The remaining two men continued to advance, firing their automatic weapons in a shower of bullets in Norm's direction. At least one bullet hit him in the chest lifting him off the ground and slamming him into the weeds.

"Take them out!" I shouted to Mark. The turret mounted mini Gatling gun sprayed both men at ten rounds per second resulting in both bodies being disintegrated.

As the men fell, our War Wagon was rocked by a blast from an approaching APC. Our enhanced armor saved us but it felt like we were inside a church bell and somebody was ringing it.

Mark returned fire with a salvo of four rockets. Three found their target. Unfortunately the APC, not equipped with enhanced armor, was reduced to a burning pile of metal and men. One man managed to escape the smoldering pile of debris. He was badly burned and collapsed about fifteen yards from the wreckage.

I called Simone to check the status of Pham.

"He's still unconscious," she replied. "I gave him a shot of morphine to dull the pain and his vitals are gradually improving. He really needs to get to a hospital ASAP."

"Can you leave him for a few minutes? We may have a prisoner and I'd love to interrogate him if he's alive," I replied.

"Roger that," she said. "I'll be there in a minute."

I saw her running around the hangar with her med kit in hand and I pointed to where the enemy soldier was lying. While she examined him, Mark did a quick scan for more bogies but none were found. We immediately drove to Norm to check him out.

He was writhing on the ground, swearing up a blue streak. "I killed one of them assholes, but the other two got me. I hurt all over, am I going to die?"

I answered, "Everyone dies eventually but you're not going to die today. Your body armor saved you. But you're going to be really sore for a while."

While I helped Norm to his feet, Simone joined us. "He's gone. He died shortly after I got to him. He was covered in third degree burns over most of his bodies. I think the burn trauma did him in."

I called in a hospital chopper to fly Norm and Pham to the closest trauma center. Simone checked Norm out while we waited for the helicopter and recommended he be checked out by a trauma doctor. Norm objected at first until Simone tapped him on the site where the bullet had imbedded itself into his body armor. His knees buckled and his face turned a very unusual shade of white and green as he stumbled backwards. He decided that Simone knew best. Simone went with them to help them en route to the hospital.

I called my handler to report what had happened to us but he didn't answer. I was about to hang up after the tenth ring but they finally picked up. I gave him our prearranged contact code but the person on the other end of the line didn't speak. At least not right away.

"I assume this is the great Joshua Brown calling to contact his handler. Unfortunately, he's not available. He's dead … I killed him. You and your motley crew will be joining him soon."

Before I could answer, Caleb thought to me, *I recognize that voice. He was one of the men at your debriefing in DC. He's the one that got all bent out of shape when a woman asked if you believed in divine intervention.*

I remembered him very well and asked Caleb, *Do you have his name?*

Of course I do. He's Senator Ralph Higgins from Arizona.

I said into the phone, "You know senator, every step of the way, you've underestimated us. You think we don't know who you are but we've been on to you and your so-called Panama soldiers. Every time they show up, we take them out. So, Senator Ralph Higgins, it's us who will continue to do the killing, not you and your ineffectual clowns you think are soldiers. You better find a good place to hide because we just successfully finished our mission and we will be coming for you next."

Somewhere during my reply, the good senator from Arizona had hung up on me. That just made me want to kill him more. I looked over at Mark who had been listening to my phone call.

He had a quizzical expression on his face. "How did you know the senator was behind the Panama cartel?"

"I didn't know for sure but Pham suggested it might be one of the people I had debriefed almost a year ago. He gave me the names of a few possibilities, and the senator from Arizona seemed the most likely candidate. Based on his reaction, I'm pretty sure I was right."

You are such a liar. Have you no shame? Lying to you own troops! Caleb chided me.

What should I have told them, that I got the intel from the spirit of my dead twin brother?

Well, thought Caleb, *when you put it that way, I guess it was the right thing to do.*

On the Road Again—Joshua

I wanted to get to DC as fast as we could. I decided we couldn't take any type of commercial or military rides. The senator or one of his friends had probably notified the local police to watch for us at all the airports, train stations and the like. Mark and I agreed we should take the War Wagon to DC. It was probably the safest way to get to capital city avoiding any barriers the senator might be using to capture us or most likely kill us.

Mark, Sarge and I left the hangar battle area and drove to the US Navy Supply Depot in New Orleans to restock and rearm the War Wagon. The last night of Mardi Gras was in full swing and we had to make several course changes to avoid the party revelers. Before we left the supply depot, Mark began programming the autopilot feature on the War Wagon. We wanted max speed but at the same time we wanted to stay on the back roads as much as possible to avoid any road blocks or highway patrol. While Mark was busy, Caleb contacted me.

Joshua, I really need to talk to you. It's very important, so please don't interrupt. I may have only a short time left.

Wow! You're scaring me, bro. What...

Don't interrupt me. If I have more time left after I finish what I have to say, ask your questions then, okay?

Okay, I replied.

When I was being shielded from accessing El Mayo's plans, I needed help to get my spirit abilities back. Without them I was afraid we wouldn't be able to complete our mission. And the mission always comes first. So I made a deal with the judge spirit. If he restored my abilities and got rid of the shield, I would have twenty-four hours before I would have to forfeit my existence. That twenty-four hours is almost up.

No! You can't do that. We're a team, Caleb. None of this works without you being with me.

It was the only way I could be sure we would complete the mission, he insisted.

The hell with the mission. I need you. You can't do…

It's already done, Josh. But before I go, I'm going to give you a data dump of everything I know about the senator, the mole inside Homeland Security and the real purpose of the Panama Cartel. You'll also need to check out the file Pham created on the War Wagon computer. It gives all the financial details and names everyone involved. It's encrypted but you can access it by logging on to PhamPanCar with Sarge052# as the password.

He paused and I was afraid he had left me. But I could feel his emotions, his sadness as he thought to me, *I love you, Josh. It has been a privilege, an honor to serve with you on this mission. I will miss…* Then he was gone and a part of me died.

I sat stunned. This couldn't be happening to me, not now, not ever. I felt I couldn't go on, nothing mattered anymore. Then I heard or maybe I just remembered, Caleb's voice, *The mission always comes first. Suck it up, Marine. You've got work to do. This mission isn't over!*

I couldn't tell what was real anymore. I felt like I was reliving what I went through when Caleb died. I kept repeating over and over until I fell asleep, "God help me…God help me…God please help me."

I awoke with a start. I was in the passenger seat and Mark was behind the wheel as the autopilot drove us toward our nation's capital at a very high speed. "How long was I asleep?" I asked.

"A little more than an hour," Mark replied. "You okay? It sounded like you were having a hell of a dream."

"Just a battle fatigue nightmare," I lied. "I'm going to call Simone before it gets any later, then I'll swap seats with you and you can get some rest."

I called Simone on what I hoped was still a secure phone and told her what had happened with the senator and we were on our way to DC in the War Wagon. I asked her how Pham and Norm were doing. She started with Norm. "Norm's a pain in the ass but he's really upset about losing the hangar and his relic aircraft. I can't say that I blame him. Health wise he's fine, just sore."

"How about Pham?" I asked. I was really concerned how he was doing.

"Pham's improving, however he's still on the critical list. He was diagnosed with a moderate to severe concussion. He wakes up and we talk for a while then falls back to sleep. Every time he wakes up he asks the same questions and I give him the same answers. That's typical of people with concussions. The last time he woke up he said to tell you to check the War Wagon computer, that all the answers are on the computer. Does that mean anything to you?"

"Actually, it does," I replied then changed the topic, "How are you doing?"

"I'm fine, tired but not damaged. I plan on leaving the hospital tomorrow morning if Norm and Pham continue to improve. I need to check in with my DEA office in DC. Maybe we can meet up when I'm done debriefing my Washington boss."

"Sounds good," I said. "As soon as we arrive at one of our safe houses in DC, I'll let you know."

"Are you okay?" she asked. "You sound like you're sad."

"I'm fine, just a little tired," I lied. "I'll catch some sleep on the drive up."

"I'm going to take a chair nap in Pham's room. Good night Joshua, tell Mark and Sarge I said hello."

I tried to sound cheerier as I replied, "Goodnight Simone." It's hard to sound cheery when a part of you has died.

Hail to the Chief—Mark

We arrived at the outskirts of DC a little after sunrise. It took us a little less than fifteen hours to complete our trip. Actually, the heavy cloud cover kept us from seeing the sun and it looked like it could start raining at any time. It had been an uneventful trip, with very few stops for bathroom breaks and diesel fuel fill ups. Joshua was different, kind of withdrawn. I wasn't sure what was up with him but it was obvious something was bothering him. Sarge sensed it too. He had crawled up on the console between the front seats and laid his head on Joshua's lap, staring up at him with his big brown eyes. I noticed Joshua began petting his massive head and gave Sarge a very faint smile but then quickly withdrew into himself.

There were several safe house locations in the DC area. Joshua, the old, original Joshua was back. He was all business now. Whatever had been bothering him he had put behind him and he was focused on our new mission. He suggested the War Wagon might be a dead give away to anyone looking for us. I agreed and kept my eyes opened for a potential secure area to stash our ride.

It was still early and traffic was very light when I discovered one of the new parking garages which looked like a vending machine. We drove into an empty box, paid our fare, took our receipt and watched as the box with the War Wagon rotated up and another empty box took its place.

Before we left the wagon, we removed our heavy body armor and settled for the lighter, less detectable vests. We also stashed all the heavy-duty weapons away into the wagon's weapons storage bins. Of course, Joshua kept his two Desert Eagles and I took my 44 Magnum semiautomatic. I also kept my 38 stub-nose revolver in an ankle holster and an assortment of knifes. I felt next to naked.

The last thing we did before leaving the War Wagon was to activate the security system. Anyone who messed with the wagon while we were gone was in for a nasty shock. Joshua also took the laptop computer. He wanted to study Pham's file on the Panama cartel.

We hailed a cab and headed for the nearest car rental agency.

Home Sweet Home—Joshua

I drove the rental Toyota Camry to my safe house in Maryland. To the best of my knowledge, nobody knew I owned my own safe house. I didn't share that information with anyone, Mark and Sarge would be the first. It was a twenty to thirty-minute drive from the safe house to the Hart Senate Office Building where Senator Harkins and his staff had their offices.

I parked the rental car in the attached garage and used an app on a burner phone to close the door. I entered the code for the rear door to the house and entered with Mark and Sarge and made a quick search of all the rooms including the basement. It appeared clear but Mark made a sweep of the entire house looking for bugs. Sarge made his own search and discovered my weapon stash but no illegal drugs were found (thank heaven).

Once we were pretty sure the house was secure, Mark sent Sarge to check out the neighborhood for anything suspicious. While Sarge was making his rounds, I opened up the computer and accessed the PhamPanCar file. It was all there. Everything I had hoped for: names, dates and financial records. He left me a note saying he had forwarded the file to the Attorney General's office requesting federal arrest warrants be issued for all the parties involved. He also suggested once the arrests were made, I should send the files to local and national news services.

I placed a call to the US Marshals Headquarters in DC using my burner phone so it couldn't be traced to me. "Hello, this is special agent Isaiah Jones from Homeland Security. I was the SAC for the Mardi Gras drug cartel bust in New Orleans a couple of days ago. I was informed by one of my agents the Attorney General's office received requests for federal arrest warrants for some very high-level government people. Can you tell me the status of those requests?"

A woman's voice replied, "I'm sorry, special agent Jones. I'm not permitted to give out that information. You'd have to come to our office so we can determine you are who you say you are. By the way, congratulations for the capture of all those drug cartel people, almost three hundred arrests in one day. That's incredible. That's going to put a huge dent in the illegal drug business. Do you think you could come in this afternoon, I'm sure we'll be able to inform you of the status of the arrest warrants."

I made an appointment to meet at their office at 1400 hours.

Mark had been listening to the call. "Does this sound like a setup to you? It smells bad to me. I think Sarge and I should accompany you to the meeting. How about we go an hour earlier and check it out?"

Welcome to My Parlor said the Spider to the Fly— Joshua

The US Marshals Headquarters is located in Arlington, Virginia, in the Crystal City Shops complex. We parked the car a couple of blocks away and the three of us walked around the shops looking for anything that was suspicious. Sarge was wearing his therapy vest and attracted a lot of attention. The building where the Marshals Headquarters was located had a twenty-foot covered walkway that ran in front of the building and wrapped around one side. The ground floor of the building had floor to ceiling windows with several double glass doors leading to an expansive lobby area. The building housed a number of businesses, including restaurants, attorneys' offices, boutiques, a medical center, dentists and several other businesses besides the US Marshals Headquarters. Mark commented there were several tall buildings with windows facing opposite the entrances, any one of which could be used by one or more snipers to target us entering or more likely, leaving the building.

"How about we walk around the building to see if there's other entrances that don't offer good sniper locations," I replied to Mark. We casually walked across the street and paused to let a tourist family make a fuss over Sarge who seemed to really enjoy his role as a therapy dog. When the family left we continued walking along around the side of the building to the back where there was a large parking garage. We noticed there were two entrance driveways, one was automated, the other had an armed guard and a sign over the entrance which read US Marshal HQ Only. We watched as a Tesla S Model drove into the secured entrance. The guard came out of his guard shack to check the credentials of the driver. Once approved, the gate was raised and the car drove in.

"Look over there," I gestured to what looked like an entrance to an escalator. "They have a subway stop underground. Let's check to see if the Marshals HQ has an entrance down there."

We took the down escalator and ended up on a large subway platform. There was a kiosk with newspapers, magazines, junk food and soft drinks located in one corner of the platform. There were also walkways to different escalators leading in and out of the subway station. More importantly, there was another entrance to the Marshals Headquarters.

We watched as a train stopped at the platform and several people got off, most heading to one of the various exit escalators. A few stopped by the kiosk, then also exited the station. Five or six people headed to the Marshals HQ entrance, badges out, ready to be scanned in. There were two armed guards who checked bags and purses for any weapons.

We waited until the guards were done with their checks. A recorded voice next to the subway tracks announced the train would be leaving in three minutes. The people who had waited for the passengers to exit, now entered the train. Two men and a woman came running down the escalator and were able to get on board just as the doors closed behind them. As the train began accelerating away to its next stop, Mark, Sarge and I walked over to the Marshals HQ guards.

I pulled out my cred pack which said I was an agent in good standing with Homeland Security and said, "Good afternoon, gentlemen. My name is Isaiah Jones and this is Mark O'Riley and his therapy dog, Sarge. We are Homeland agents and have a meeting scheduled in a few minutes, can we enter here?"

The younger guard had squatted down in front of Sarge and asked Mark if it was okay to pet Sarge. Mark nodded and the guard began petting him as the other guard answered my question.

"Sorry sir, this entrance is for badged employees only. You're going to have to go upstairs to check in. They should have your names on the approved visitors list. However, you can leave from this location when your meeting is finished if that would be convenient for you."

I thanked them for their time and we headed back upstairs. Our meeting was scheduled to begin in about ten minutes and just like the HQ guard said, our names were on the approved visitors list, Sarge included.

Two agents, a man and a woman, escorted us to an elevator dedicated for Marshals HQ staff. When the elevator stopped on the nineteenth floor and the doors opened, we were greeted by applause from the entire HQ staff and agents. There was even a banner, with Welcome, Heroes of the Largest Drug Bust Ever!! What a great surprise!

A middle-aged woman in a business suit stepped forward and offered her hand which Mark and I both shook as she introduced herself. "Agents, I'm Assistant Marshal Brenda Craig, my boss, Marshal Thomas Blake, couldn't be with us today. He's busy serving the arrest warrants we received yesterday from the Attorney General's office. He asked me to pass on his congratulations to you and your staff for a job well done, very well done. With the arrest of Senator Higgins and Assistant Deputy Secretary of Homeland Security Graham and all the other government officials involved, this mission is officially closed."

There was more applause as Assistant Marshal Craig escorted us to her office to give me the list of all the government people involved in this 'heinous crime' (her words, not mine). The list had almost a hundred government employees named along with the criminal activities they were involved with. She went on to say, "I understand your agent who provided the information that led to those arrests was severely injured."

"That's correct, Assistant Mar…" I began.

"Call me Brenda, please," she interrupted.

"The agent's name is Pham Bin Mihn, Brenda, and he suffered a severe concussion caused by the attack of the so-called Panama cartel. They were really American mercenaries hired to keep us from finding out the government's plans to profit from the cartels' drug sales."

"How is he doing?" she asked.

"He's still in the hospital but he's slowly recovering," I answered.

"Please give him my condolences for his injuries but also congratulate him on his outstanding work putting this all together." She paused briefly, to look at a text message.

"I'm sorry, gentlemen but I have to take care of some urgent business. Please let all of your people know how proud we are of what they accomplished. One of our agents will escort you out."

The female agent who had escorted us in also took us to the elevator and down to the subway platform. As we began walking toward the escalator to take us to the surface, we noticed three things: the two HQ guards were missing; there was a different man working at the kiosk, a very large, mean looking man and the train was stationary at the platform with its lights out, doors wide open and nobody inside that we could see. In fact, the platform was empty except for us and large, mean-looking kiosk man.

Mark wasted no time. "Sarge attack."

The wolf-dog didn't hesitate, Mark barely got his leash off before Sarge took off like a bullet fired at mean-looking kiosk man. The man pulled out two hand guns from behind his back but before he could fire either weapon, Sarge was on him. He jumped high into the air and hit the man in the chest knocking him and the kiosk backwards, crashing to the floor. Both guns went clattering to the concrete as the man tried to push Sarge off of him. Sarge wouldn't be denied, he grabbed the man by the throat and bit through his neck. Blood began shooting out from both carotid arteries. He struggled briefly, then went limp, his breathing stopped, his eyes wide open and glazed over.

Mark and I focused on the subway train. Mark was holding his 44 Magnum in both hands as he moved toward the rear of the train while I held both of my Desert Eagles, one in each hand. I heard movement in the front of an opened train car door and began moving in that direction.

Mark yelled out, "Shooter!" and dove behind one of the many support columns as shots rang out from the open doors of the next-to-last train car. He returned fire from his Magnum and pulled the 32-snub nose from his ankle holster. He yelled a command at Sarge in what I think was German and the wolf-dog sprinted towards the opened doors in the last car. Once inside he moved slowly and cautiously up the aisle of the train car.

The shooter screamed in pain as he bolted out of the train onto the platform, bleeding from extensive bite wounds. He was backing away, his pistol aimed at the open door, waiting for Sarge to come at him again. Mark stood up and yelled, "Hey! Over here."

The man turned and Mark shot him between the eyes, lifting him off his feet and slamming him to the concrete floor. Sarge slowly walked out of the car, looking for more game to hunt. When he couldn't find any, he walked over to the dead shooter, lifted his hind leg and marked his territory.

I was waiting behind a support column close to the forward end of the train and sang to them, "Come out, come out wherever you are. It's time to come out and play. It's time for you to come out, I really don't have all day."

Two men appeared in different doors and began spraying the area with Uzi machine pistols. Mark was lying on the concrete floor behind a column and returned fire at the closest bogey. Sarge darted back into the train and began working his way forward for another attack.

I waited until my target had emptied his magazine before stepping out from behind my column and shot him in both eyes.

The force of the bullets lifted him off the ground and dropped him half in and half out of the open door of the train car.

We waited to see if Sarge could find any more bad guys. A few minutes later he strolled out of the front car and trotted over to Mark who gave him a big hug and told him what a good boy he was.

The train was clear.

We heard sirens in the background as the door to Marshals HQ opened and the young woman who had escorted us came running out with a Glock held in both hands, scanning for anymore targets. I turned back to Mark to signal all clear when I heard someone yell, "Watch out!"

Everything was a blur after that.

I remember hearing several gun shots and feeling like somebody had hit me in my neck with a sledge hammer. I heard people screaming and more shots, then nothing as I slowly slid down the column and sprawled out onto the concrete floor.

My last thoughts were, *I'm dying. This really sucks.*

Resurrection—Caleb

I had been whisked away from Joshua right in the middle of a sentence. I was standing on what looked like a cloud with what appeared to be my old, pre-blown up body looking at Judge Joaquin Castelán. He was sitting behind a judge's bench wearing his black judge's robe.

"Hello, your Honor. Is it time for you to take my pound of flesh?"

He gave me a stern look and answered, "First, don't call me your Honor. You may call me judge. Secondly, you are a spirit, you don't have a pound of flesh for me to take."

"I was speaking metaphorically," I replied.

"Do tell," the judge replied.

"Is this going to hurt? Like being thrown into a lake of fire to burn forever for my sins?"

"Will you please shut up so I can tell you what I have to tell you? Honestly, you don't know when to keep your mouth shut and listen. Do you think I don't have any other spirits to judge? My docket is full and I … Excuse me, I digress but you're something of an enigma."

I remained silent, waiting for the other shoe to fall (another metaphor, sorry).

"Those who are my superiors in all things have decided your fate. Your existence will not be extinguished. You will not be immortal, at least not yet, but you may live for many centuries."

I was so shocked by his words I couldn't help myself and blurted out, "So I'm to become a judge like you? That's so co…"

He picked up a gavel and pounded it down on the block and shouted at me, "For heaven's sake! No! Not like me. Not even close." He composed himself and continued. "You will have very specific missions to carry out. Your first mission will be saving the life of your brother, Joshua."

It felt like a strong lightning bolt had just struck my pretend body. "Joshua is dying? Send me to him. Tell me how to save him. Quit wasting time…"

The gavel slammed down again and I found he had removed my mouth. "Time is a construct. You and I could be together for years and not one second would have passed in what you called reality. I shudder at that visual. You can also go forward or back in time as needed but please, please don't abuse that privilege, it can lead to so many contradictions. When you enter back into reality, your brother will have been shot in the neck and is bleeding out. One of the bullets remains lodged in his neck next to his spinal column. Doctors will be reluctant to operate for fear of nerve damage which would leave him paralyzed. Your immediate mission is to fix him. Understand?"

I nodded my head.

"Excellent. Case dismissed, call if you need help."

He was gone and my consciousness materialized in a subway station with bodies and blood everywhere.

I stopped time, at least from my perspective time stopped, and I took my time checking out everything.

My poor brother, he was unconscious and had lost a lot of blood, *I'm back, Joshua. Everything will be all right. I can't make this look like a miracle but you are going to live. Eventually, you'll be as good as new. I will never leave you again. Together we will make those who hurt you pay for what they have done.*

Doctor, Doctor Tell Me the News—Caleb

The EMT managed to stop Joshua's bleeding. Of course I contributed by lowering his heart rate and redirecting his blood flow to bypass the injured blood vessels. With the gifts I was given, I could have made a fortune as a surgeon, just a passing thought.

The bullet lodged next to his spine was not going to be an easy fix. I did my best to cushion the ambulance ride on the way to the hospital and manipulated traffic to prevent any fast maneuvers by our driver.

Once at the hospital, he was rushed into the ER and the medical team went to work. I was able to monitor all of his vital signs and tweak them before anyone noticed any drift. They isolated his head and neck to prevent any movement of the bullet then went to work on the damaged blood vessels. During the ride in the ambulance I had accelerated the healing process and I estimated they were almost completely repaired.

The lead surgeon commented after checking out the wound, "I thought the EMT said the blood vessels in his neck were badly damaged. It doesn't look that way to me." He gestured to his surgical nurse. "What do you think, Carmen?"

The nurse looked over his shoulder and nodded her agreement. "I know he's lost a lot of blood but not from the vessels in his neck. There's hardly any blood oozing. Any indication of internal bleeding?"

"None," the assisting doctor said.

As they watched they could almost see the wounds closing of their own accord, with my help of course. Within an hour, you couldn't tell he ever had a wound in his neck except for the slight scarring.

The doctor shook his head and commented, "This borders on miraculous healing. I've never seen or even heard of a gunshot wound healing so fast. We got video on this don't we?"

The med tech nodded his head. "This is going to make for a great paper for the Journal of Advanced Medicine. What's been happening to the bullet lodged next to his spine?"

While the medical team was fussing over the rapid healing of the blood vessels, I had been focusing on the bullet. The bullet had been designed to fragment into multiple sharp pieces inside the body and that's exactly what it did. There were at least four major fragments, three of which were touching the vertebrae in Joshua's neck. The fourth one was actually wedged between two vertebrae, within millimeters of the spinal column.

I began by eliminating the sharp, jagged edges. When I began to back the fragments out so they wouldn't damage the muscle tissue, pushing past small capillaries and nerves along the way.

The next step was to cause the muscle in his neck to back out the fragments. It was kind of like peristaltic contractions that occur in the digestive system to move the body's waste down and out the colon. Without it, it would be impossible to poop.

One fragment at a time, I caused the neck muscles to contract in the proper sequence forcing metal to back out the entry path. There was a metallic clank when the first fragment fell onto the operating table.

"What was that?" asked the doctor. He had been conferencing with the med team on how best to remove the bullet fragments.

One of the nurses answered, "It looks like one of the bullet fragments fell out of his neck."

"That's impossible," he said as he moved back to the table. As he watched, one by one all the fragments plopped out of the entrance wound which closed abruptly after the last fragment was out. "Has anyone ever seen this happen before?" he asked.

Another doctor replied, "I just saw it happen and I still don't believe it. Is this guy some kind of self-healing alien life form?"

There was nothing left for them to do except to give Joshua a liter of blood, which I could have done myself but hey, I felt I needed to let them do something.

Ordinarily, they would have put him in ICU but they decided he didn't need that level of care. Instead they placed him in a standard patient room to convalesce.

Am I Dead? —Joshua

Where am I? What happened to me? Am I dead? Is this what being dead feels like? Maybe I'm not dead. Can I feel anything? Yes! I can feel my fingers touching something. I think it's a sheet. Am I in bed? Yes, I think I'm in a bed. I can feel my toes touching the sheet.

Are you finally waking up? It's about time! Open your eyes, Joshua. It's me. It's Caleb.

But you're gone, gone forever. It's not really you, you're just a memory of my brother.

Oh, for crying out loud! Open your eyes, look around. You're in a hospital bed. You were shot in the neck and were mostly dead but not completely dead. Someone's coming. Don't mention me to anyone. They're not ready to know about me.

"I think he's finally waking up." It was a woman's voice. A familiar voice. Simone's? Maybe Simone's voice. But why is she licking my face?

"Down Sarge, Joshua will open his eyes soon. You don't have to wake him up." A man's voice. It was Mark, I'm sure of it. It must have been his dog licking me.

I have to open my eyes. I felt my eyes lids begin fluttering, why was it so difficult to open my eyes?

The light was very bright and I had to keep blinking to get adjusted to seeing again. In the brief instances of clarity, I could see glimpses of two people, a man and a woman. It was Mark and Simone, I'm sure of it. And Sarge was there too. I need to talk to them, to find out what happened to me.

It's me Caleb, again. I'll fill in the details later. Just say hello.

I could see them more clearly now. I tried really hard to smile but wasn't sure if I made it. "Hello you two." I sounded like a croaking frog. Is a croaking frog one that's dying? I tried again, "Hi Mark, where's Sarge? Oh, there he is. Hi, big guy. Good to see you. And Simone, you look as beautiful as ever. Give me a kiss."

She giggled, leaned over and kissed me on the mouth. "Welcome back, Joshua or is it Isaiah or maybe Clarence?"

I felt a strange sense of urgency. "I think I have to pee." I pushed the call button for a nurse. He wouldn't let me up until he removed my catheter. How embarrassing and what a strange feeling. "Help me up please."

Mark stepped in and managed to get me to a standing position and walked me into the bathroom. I felt much better after I had relieved myself. All of a sudden, I felt like I had received a shot of adrenalin. I felt strong and alert. *Caleb, what did you do?*

Just helpin' a brother out. That's all.

"I need to get out of here, where are my clothes?"

"Whoa," said the nurse. "You aren't going anywhere until your doctor releases you. Have a seat and I'll take your vitals. If you're up to snuff, I'll call your doctor."

As he did his probing and prodding, I asked Simone, "Where are we? Are we still in DC?"

"Yes we are," she answered. "Pham and Norm were released a few days ago. They're on their way to join us here."

I was glad to hear they were recovered enough to travel but then frowned. "Just how long was I unconscious?"

"Nearly a week," Mark replied. "You needed complete rest to regain your strength. It seems to have worked."

Caleb! I thought shouted. *Why didn't you use the powers your fairy God Father gave you and get me out of here sooner?*

We had to keep up appearances. Some of the doctors already think you're some sort of alien superman, Caleb thought back to me. *A lot has happened since you were wounded. We'll fill you in on the details once we get out of here.*

The on-call doctor checked my vitals (again) and signed off on me leaving. An hour later we were back at the safe house in Maryland.

How Safe is the Safe House? —Joshua

Mark drove the rental car from the hospital to the Maryland safe house. In light of what had happened, it took him twice as long and lots of strange turns to make sure we weren't being tailed before driving into the garage and parking next to the War Wagon.

Simone sat in the passenger seat and I was in the back with Sarge. Simone and Mark made a very thorough search of the house while Sarge scouted the outside property. I remained in the car until we gave me the all clear.

Once inside, Mark turned on the jammer and we all sat down in the living room. I assumed things had changed and not for the better. "So, what's happened after I got shot? Are we still the good guys?"

"Barely," answered Mark and Simone nodded her head in agreement. "Since Sarge and I were with you in the subway station, let me bring you up to speed."

A voice in my head added, *I'll offer my perspective when we're alone.*

Thanks, Caleb, I replied silently.

Mark began. "When you went down, Sarge took out the marshal who shot you. The same woman who escorted us down the elevator and dropped us at the subway station is the one who shot you. She had backup, two additional marshals fired at me and Sarge. I shot one of them before an army of marshals exploded onto the platform. They said you and I were under arrest for the murder of three innocent civilians and two marshals."

"It was a set up? After all the applause, the hero banner and the admiration of Assistant Marshal Brenda, it was a set up?"

"Yes indeed. The only reason you weren't left to die and Sarge and I weren't arrested on the spot, was my passing comment that I had recorded the entire shootout on my body cam and sent a copy to the FBI, Attorney General and every local and national news outlet I could think of."

"Was that a bluff?" I asked dumbfounded.

"Of course not," answered Mark. "Bluffing was not an option. I had my body cam tied into all those people at Pham's suggestion before the Sinaloa cartel party. Don't you have the same feature on your body cam?"

I thought hard. "Yeah, I guess I do. Ain't technology grand?"

"Anyway, since that showdown, we are considered *persona non grata* at the Marshals HQ. I'm pretty sure they haven't given up trying to make us the bad guys. They're probably hidden away somewhere planning more dastardly deeds."

A phone rang and Simone picked up one of her burner phones and just listened. After a moment, she said, "Roger that."

"That was Pham and Norm, they said they will be joining us as soon as it's safe. They're going to change their rides but plan to show up after dark. Why don't we hold off with any further discussion until they arrive so we don't have to repeat ourselves. I'm hungry, who wants lunch?"

It was strange, I hadn't felt hungry until Simone mentioned lunch. I wondered if Caleb was messing with me. I got immediate feedback.

You need to eat, bro. You've been living on IVs for several days and have dropped some of your massively muscular physique.

When they gave you all these new abilities did they also turn you into my mother?

Hee hee, that's a real knee slapper, Josh. However, the last time I checked, I was still all man.

You're spirit, not flesh. You got nothing to check.

Au contraire, monsieur, the image I have of myself is definitely masculine. And I don't change with age. While you, on the other hand…

Simone thankfully interrupted our banter. "Lunch is ready. Help yourselves."

I have to admit, regardless of the source, I did feel hungry. I had decent helpings of everything on the counter, which is the way I describe having seconds and the occasional third.

I felt comfortably full and thought I should hit the weights in the basement. My biggest dread was wasting away so lifting some heavy iron would be a good start. I opened the door to the basement and started down. Somehow, I suddenly felt very fatigued and decided a nap would be better. As I laid down, I knew without any doubt, Caleb had caused this but I was too tired to care. A few minutes later I was sound asleep.

I awoke with a start (a lot of that going on lately). There was a knock on the front door. I grabbed one of the Desert Eagles from under my pillow and walked out of the bedroom just in time to see Mark open the front door. Two men I had never seen before walked in and I raised my gun.

Simone yelled, "Hold it, Joshua! It's Pham and Norm."

I lowered my gun and my mouth fell open in complete surprise. The one on the right said as he began pulling his mask off of his head. "That Mission Impossible mask machine is a real hoot!"

Big Trouble in River City—Pham

It was so good to see Joshua again, especially after I took my mask off. Unfortunately, what I had to tell him wasn't very encouraging. In fact, it was downright depressing.

"The arrest warrants for Senator Higgins and Assistant Deputy Secretary Graham from Homeland Security were never issued. Neither was the one for Deputy Marshal Brenda Craig. The Attorney General's office was in complete disarray. I haven't been able to reach my contact there. Everyone I speak with denies even knowing him. As far as the media is concerned, mums the word. It's like the Sinaloa mission never existed."

"What about all the cartel people who were arrested in New Orleans?" Joshua asked.

"They're still in lock up but I've heard rumors most of the charges are going to be dropped. Of course, the Sinaloa cartel leadership are all dead but there are other rumors they will be replaced by the Panama cartel which is really being run by our own government. There's so much money at stake everybody wants a piece of it, or more accurately, they want the whole enchilada. They don't want to shut down the illegal drug business, they want to own it."

Joshua seemed like he was in a trance, as if he were listening to someone speaking the rest of us couldn't hear. Everyone was staring at him. Simone broke the silence. "Joshua, are you okay?"

He seemed to snap out of it. "Sorry," he said. "Pham do you know how many government people are running this operation?"

"I estimate no more than six."

"Do you know all their names?" Joshua asked.

"Sure," I said and wrote the names and titles of the six people I believed were leading this coup. "What are you going to do?"

"I think we need to have a serious talk with each of these people. They need to be informed of the error of their ways," he answered.

Mark jumped in. "Are you serious, Joshua? Those six people would have so many layers of protection, there's no way we could get close to them. It would be suicide to try."

He ignored Mark's comments and said, "We need to do this as soon as possible. The people I used to work for are probably already dead. Our organization is crumbling. It's only a matter of time before they locate us." He stopped speaking and got that far away look in his eyes again. A moment later he said, "I need to sleep on this. See you all in the morning. Good night."

With that, he turned and walked back into his bedroom and closed and locked the door.

We all sat stunned at his strange behavior. Simone asked Mark, "Do you think he's having some type of breakdown?"

"I have no idea," he said as he shrugged his shoulder and looked at his watch. "It's late. I guess we should go to bed and see what happens tomorrow."

The Final Plan—Joshua

*A*re *you sure you can do what you told me?*

Absolutely," he answered. *I'm not bragging, I know exactly what needs to be done and how to do it. It will all be over by tomorrow morning.*

How can I help you? I asked.

You can't, bro. Only a spirit can do what I suggested. Just go to sleep and I guarantee everything will be better tomorrow morning when you get up. You're probably feeling pretty tired right now. Why don't you lay down and go to sleep?

He was right, I did feel tired. I could hardly keep my eyes opened as I stumbled into bed.

I was fast asleep as soon as my head hit the pillow.

You've Been Very Bad Boys and Girls—Caleb

One by one I visited each of the six names Pham had given to Joshua. It took me less than an hour with each of them. I made them realize how bad they had been and how they should be punished for their sins. What they were doing was terrible. The number of people they had hurt or had killed was indefensible.

Of course they tried to rationalize their behavior, they were above the law and the things they did was for the greater good but they soon came to realize what a lie that was. The more they resisted, the stronger I reinforced their need to be punished. Some were afraid, deathly afraid of spending the rest of their life in prison. I showed them what their life would be like in prison, how their power would be stripped from them and they would be beaten by stronger and meaner people than they were. Some couldn't bear to live that way. Eventually, they realized there was only one option open to them but first they needed to confess their sins, not only to God but to the whole world.

Each one decided to make a recording of their confession. They varied in length, depending on just how nasty, mean and rotten they had been. They said there was no possible way their sins would ever be forgiven.

When their confessions were completed, each of them took their own lives. Some took poison, others sliced open their wrists and bled out.

Senator Higgins from Arizona imagined himself as the last of the wild west cowboys. He placed a working replica of a 44-caliber cap and ball revolver from the 1800s into his mouth and blew his brains out on camera, a fitting ending to his career.

Follow the Money—Pham

The wealth of the combined cartels was estimated to be in excess of many trillions of dollars. That's right, trillions with a T. With all of the major cartel people either dead or sentenced to life in prison, you'd think the nations of the world would end up with most of those trillions. However, you'd be wrong.

Of course, some of the windfall did go to several of the larger nations in the Western Hemisphere but much of it went to expanding their prison capacity to accommodate the spike in the newly incarcerated.

So where did the bulk of all that money go?

Nobody truly knows for sure but many believe it went to charities. For some unexplainable reason, the world's financial experts weren't able to trace the money. They couldn't explain the paths the money must have followed to arrive at the numerous charities. All of the donations were made anonymously and no amount of sophisticated, high power software running on supercomputers was able to provide satisfactory answers. What a conundrum!

Many of the religious charities claimed it must be divine intervention. Others believed it was watching the news feeds showing the fate of so many high-powered politicos. They claimed it prompted people to donate ill received wealth, to make up for their not-quite-legal means of gaining that wealth.

The bottom line was nobody ever truly knew where the money came from.

There was one organization, not a charitable organization nor a non-profit company, which received a sizable yearly anonymous donation to cover its annual operating costs. The clandestine organization had no official name and had previously been funded by the United States government. However, the government funding had dried up and it transitioned to become a privately owned company.

Not much was known about the company except that they continued their clandestine operations. The agents who worked there had several aliases and multiple passports.

The only thing known for sure was their motto: Money be Damned! Do the Right Thing.

EPILOGUE

Caleb

Let me be perfectly clear, I can't force anyone to do something they really don't want to do. As a spirit, I can't physically harm anyone in anyway. Other than Joshua, I can't even communicate with them. Joshua and I are bonded together which allows us to carry on conversations with each other but I can't talk or hear. We communicate by thought projection. It's equivalent to talking without any sound. I can't have that type of communication with anyone except Joshua and he can't project his thoughts to anyone but me.

However, I can read peoples' minds. I can understand their thoughts and sense their emotions but they aren't aware I'm spying on them. Even that type of contact has limitations, the most important limitation is that my consciousness has to be in close proximity to the person or persons I want to read.

Recently, I received an upgrade to my ability. I can now select certain areas of a person's thoughts and amplify them or conversely, I can diminish them. A recent example of this has to do with the six men and women who committed suicide.

First, let me give you some background. Flesh and blood human beings are born with the ability to choose. They can choose to be good or they can choose to be evil. During their lifetimes, all people choose a combination of both. Those who occasionally do something evil and regret it are usually considered good (or righteous, if you prefer). Those who predominantly choose to do evil things and don't care whom they hurt are considered evil (the title psychopath comes to mind as well as sinner).

The six people who committed suicide were evil, sinning, psychopaths. What I did was to diminish their evil thoughts and amplify what little good thoughts they had. I made them face up to the fact they were wicked, despicable, selfish creatures with no sense of remorse for their evil ways. They had no right to continue living.

I finally got all of them to agree. It wasn't easy for the worst of them, they actually prided themselves in being evil. However, I persevered until they accepted suicide was their only option.

Some may disagree with my tampering with their right to choose to be evil. God will decide their fate and I shouldn't play the role of God. This would be my response to their comments.

God has avenging angels who have struck down many evil people. While I am no angel, I am a spirit who has been rewarded for dealing harshly with evil men and women. I may have taken their lives but God alone will be their ultimate judge. He has given me the ability to seek out and destroy the bodies of exceptionally evil people.

God alone will deal with their souls.

Joshua

Things are changing, dramatically changing. We are no longer supported by our government, in fact I'm concerned we may be considered criminals. At the present time, we have no idea of how to determine which missions we should take. We can no longer be considered special agents of any of the alphabet agencies. Any contact with them is tenuous at best.

There will be some changes to our team. Norm has decided to stay in Louisiana. He has received several substantial donations by various flying organizations, from crop dusters, airline companies and their pilots to the US Air Force. He wants to rebuild his hangar and purchase a few Stearman relics. First, he has to finish the 'barn storming tour' of TV talk shows to replay his thoughts on what he calls The Mexican-Crop Duster Battle.

Simone says she's done with the DEA and wants to remain with the team. I was very glad to hear that. She's become a very special person in my life. I just hope we'll still have a team.

Pham, Mark and even Sarge also want to stay with the team but first they would like some downtime. They have friends and families in Portland they would like to visit. A trip to Portland sounds good to me as well. I made some really good friends there, especially Pastor Bao and his wife Cam. I also want to see how all his adopted Vietnamese students are progressing.

We decided to take the War Wagon and drive to Oregon. Actually we're going to rent a very large U-Haul truck with the War Wagon inside and out of sight.

We'll take the scenic route and make it a leisurely trip. We'll follow the news to determine if our country sees us as heroes or villains.

This is Frank G. Davis. This concludes the book of <u>Joshua and Caleb</u>, the second book in the <u>Joshua</u> series. If you enjoyed the book please send me an email at:

<u>sciencefictionfrank@gmail.com</u>

and let me know what you think of the story. I promise to reply to all emails and give you updates on the next book in the series, titled <u>The Book of Caleb.</u>

About the Author

I've been a fan of science fiction ever since I was in grade school (a very long time ago). In those days there were three outstanding authors: Isaac Asimov, Arthur C. Clark, and Robert A. Heinlein.

My favorite author was Heinlein. He began writing his science fiction stories for young people. His first books were categorized as 'Boys Books.' Today, they're called 'Young Adults.' His stories were very believable to me and I couldn't wait to get to his latest books. As I matured, so did his books. I have read every book Heinlein published and still have most of them in my personal library. I think my all-time favorite Heinlein story is *Stranger in a Strange Land.*

My current favorite author is Orson Scott Card. Again, like Heinlein's stories, I find myself 'living' the story as it unfolds. *Ender's Game* and *Prentice Alvin* are two of my favorite Card novels.

I've always had an interest in writing science fiction novels. I would read books by new authors and say to myself, "I could write a better story." However, when I tried, publishers didn't agree. When Covid-19 broke out, I had a lot of spare time on my hands and decided to give it another shot.

During the last two years, I have written seven novels with an eighth one in the works. And I'm just getting started. During the last two and a half years, I have written eight novels. I plan on publishing the ninth one in 2022.

More Books From Frank G. Davis

The Generations Trilogy:

www.ingramcontent.com/pod-product-compliance
Lightning Source LLC
Chambersburg PA
CBHW071225210726
48293CB00002B/587